ROGUE DEVIL

KYLIE GILMORE

Friends to lovers is a risky path…

1

———

Three days before Christmas, Villroy Island

Chloe

"Do you think you can be friends with a guy after you've slept with him?" I ask my older sister, Sara.

"No."

I sigh and lean my head back on the cushy leather reclining chair in the living room of her suite at Amalie Palace. The palace is my home away from home ever since Sara married Prince Adrian Rourke. I can always count on her to be honest with me. Still, I don't want it to be true.

"But—" I start.

"No." She leans forward from the adjacent sofa and squeezes my hand. Her green eyes are direct. "Chloe, I know you think what you had with Michael was a friends-with-benefits arrangement, but what you actually had was a relationship."

I frown. It's been three months since I turned down Michael's proposal, which, by the way, was a complete shock. I had no idea he felt that way. He's a palace guard I met while visiting Sara, here on Villroy Island just off the coast of southwestern France. I hope we can remain friends. I'll be a regular visitor to Villroy since Sara lives here.

Sara pushes her blond hair behind her ears and continues in her motherly way. She's seven years older and raised me after our parents died. "You remember how I was before Adrian? I was so closed off, unwilling to take a chance on someone and let them into my heart. And you told me to go for it with him. Chloe, that was the best decision of my life. Look at me now, happy as I've ever been, married with a beautiful baby boy."

I swallow the lump of emotions lodged in my throat. I love that Sara is so happy. She deserves it. "I'm thrilled for you, you know that, but it's not the same situation at all. Adrian was your childhood friend. It was like destiny or something. Michael is not my destiny."

"That may be true," she says gently. "What I'm trying to say is that even though the external circumstances are different with our situations, on the inside you and I are very much the same. Because of what happened with Mom and—"

I hold up a palm. "This has nothing to do with them." I barely remember our parents because they died when I was only six. I secretly think I'm broken. I never cry. Even when my parents died, I didn't. Sara says I went mute for three months instead. And I didn't love Michael back, even though he's a good guy.

She sighs. "Okay. I just want to encourage you to open up a little. You tend to shut down." Her brows draw together. "I'm afraid I set a bad example for you the way I didn't connect with other people in a meaningful way for so long. I want better for you. You're a caring person with a lot of love to give."

"I love Henry." That's my baby nephew, her son.

She smiles. "I know you do, but he's too little to contribute to your social life."

I laugh.

She wags a finger, saying in a light tone, "Even serious students are allowed to have a boyfriend. It's called work-life balance, and sometimes that means taking a risk when the *right* person comes along. No matter how scary it feels."

I straighten in my seat. I'm not scared. Sara didn't go to

college, so she doesn't understand the pressure. I'm double majoring in biology and chemistry at Columbia University in New York City on an accelerated path to graduate in three years, and then I'm off to medical school. I always knew doing what I was born to do, ultimately becoming a medical researcher, would mean I had to make some sacrifices. Long hours and hard work are part of the deal. I just never wanted anyone else to get hurt because of it.

The door to the suite opens. My brother-in-law, Adrian, strides in, holding my three-month-old nephew, Henry. Adrian is tall with dark brown hair, warm hazel eyes, and the classic Rourke angular cheekbones and square jaw. "He's hungry," he says to Sara.

"Aww, hi, Henry!" I say. I met him the day after he was born, back in September, and now we're reunited again. He pays no attention to me. He's fussing in Adrian's arms, screwing up his little face in preparation for a major cry session.

Sara rapidly undoes the buttons on her blouse and holds her arms out to him. Adrian transfers the baby over to nurse. The three of them sit close together on the sofa. My throat tightens, taking in their loving family. I can't help but feel like an outsider. It used to be just me and Sara against the world.

I stand. "I'll see you later."

Sara looks up. "Will you be returning to the ball? You look so pretty in that gown. The color is such a nice contrast with your hair and really brings out your eyes." Sara and I look similar, blond hair and green eyes, except I recently dyed my hair red.

"Thanks." I glance down at the green empire-waist gown my sister-in-law had made for me. It's a Regency-themed ball, so we all had to go in proper Regency-era attire. "I only went to the ball because Queen Anna wanted me there. I don't enjoy dancing, and the dances they were doing looked complicated." I wave my hand through the air like a snake. "Lines of dancers weaving in and out of each other, turning this way and that."

Sara smiles. "It sounds fun. I hope we do another

Christmas ball next year. Then we can take Henry." Adrian felt it was too soon for Henry to be exposed to so many germs.

"I'll make sure of it," Adrian says, kissing her temple.

They gaze into each other's eyes, the love between them palpable.

"Bye," I mumble and see myself out, quietly shutting the door behind me.

I head downstairs on heavy limbs to my guest room on the second floor. I plan to change and get back to studying for the MCAT. That's the admissions test for medical school that I'm taking this spring. From now on, work will be my focus. Even friends with benefits is more than I can handle. Obviously, I'm terrible at relationships. I didn't even know I was in one until he proposed. From here on out, I'm steering clear of relationships of any kind so no one gets hurt.

It's afternoon on Christmas Day, and I'm curled up in a plush chair in my room, reading the latest in *The New England Journal of Medicine* on my laptop. Except for the Christmas morning gift-giving festivities, I've mostly stayed in my room, reading medical journals and studying. Usually, reading is a relaxing break for me, but today I'm restless.

I look over at my little troll doll, Kablooey, with his blue explosion of hair, perched on the end table. I picked him up at a flea market years ago, and he travels with me everywhere for good luck. "I'm thinking cookie time, how about you?"

His wide smile remains in place.

Looks like a yes to me.

I set my laptop aside, stand, and stretch before making my way downstairs to the kitchen, where a couple of servants are cleaning up from brunch. "Hi, Eileen, do you still have those cookie cutters in the shape of music notes?"

Eileen, a middle-aged woman with her hair in a brown bob, smiles. "Sure do, Miss Chloe. Would you like some for Christmas dessert? I'll whip up a batch right now."

"Would it be okay if I made them?" I've done it before while visiting, so it's not that unusual a request.

She waves me forward. "Of course. Just be done by three because that's when Chef comes back to start preparations for dinner."

I thank her and get to work. I could make sugar cookies in my sleep. These will be a friendly peace offering to musically inclined Michael.

Once I finish, I borrow one of the old Renaults the servants drive around the island and head down the hill to Michael's cottage. His car isn't in the driveway. I text him to ask where he is, but there's no reply. I call and it goes to voice-mail. I'm not sure if he's blocked my number or if he turned his phone off. The sun's just starting to set, so I need to work quickly before I lose the light.

Determined to see this through, I retrieve the large plastic container of cookies from where I carefully wedged it on the floor of the passenger seat and make my way to the music room on the side of the cottage. He goes in there every day, and I happen to know the window doesn't latch properly. It's broken and he never got around to getting a new one installed. I wiggle the metal frame and push it up as far as I can, which is not a lot. I'm short and need a little height to get it open the rest of the way. I was planning to set the cookies on the bookcase under the window, but they won't fit through this small opening.

I think for a moment about how to achieve my goal. *I got it!* I walk over to the front porch, set the cookies down, and grab a nearby terracotta planter with a miniature pine tree he put out for Christmas. I drag the planter over and set it under the window. There's just enough room around the skinny tree for my feet. I go back for the cookies. Okay, I can do this. I hold the cookie container in one hand, use the other hand on the windowsill for balance, and step into the planter's soil. *Whoa.* My feet just sank all the way to my ankles. My poor white Keds are now brown. He must've recently watered it.

Okay, I can still make this work. I've got a little height now. I push the window open more and carefully slide the container through the opening onto the top of the bookcase. Then I pull my planned speech from my front jeans pocket and place it under the container. I came up with my speech while the cookies were baking, and wrote it down to be sure I got the words just right. I'm so glad I did because now it's the perfect friendly note.

I'm about to step out of the planter when a sudden bout of nerves has me frozen in place, staring at that note. I snatch it back, pull my phone from my back jeans pocket, and turn on the flashlight to read it, ignoring the damp leaching into my socks from the planter. My note is short and to the point: I *never meant to hurt you. I hope we can be friends.*

I debate if I need to find a pen to add my name to it. Maybe there's a pen in the glove compartment of the car. I didn't go back to my room for my purse since I didn't figure I'd need it. I glance over at the car just in time to see it rolling down the hill. *Shit!* I shove the note and phone back in my pockets and step out of the planter. One of my feet gets caught on the damn plant and the whole thing tips, tossing me to the ground. *Oof.*

Okay, nothing broken. I jump up and race after the car.

"Wait! Stop!" *What am I saying?* There's no one driving it.

I run, waving wildly for the car to stop. Like I have some magical power to reverse gravity. I must've forgot to put the emergency brake on. I'm not used to driving much, living in the city.

Please don't hit another cottage.

The road curves to the left, but the car doesn't. It keeps going, heading for a cliff. *Oh no. No, no, no.* I slap my hands over my mouth and watch in horror. *Reverse! Reverse!*

The car grinds to a stop, halfway over the cliff, tangled in the native shrubbery. I blow out a breath of relief and catch up to it. At least no people or cottages are in danger. It's just beach down below.

I take in all the angles, considering if there's any way for me to get the car safely back up or down. Nope. It needs a tow. I sigh, my shoulders slumping.

I turn and trudge back uphill to his cottage. At least I can deliver my note.

I right the planter, and then I have to use my hands to scoop the soil back into it and compact it enough for me to have a sturdy surface to climb back in. *Okay, once more with feeling.* I wipe my hands clean on my jeans, haul myself back to the window ledge, and slide the note under the cookie container.

I swallow over the lump in my throat, shut the window, carefully step out of the planter, and drag it back to the front porch.

I take one last look at the cottage—my warm and happy oasis once upon a time—and turn away. The palace is at the top of a long, winding road. I consider calling for a ride, but I don't want this getting back to Sara. She'll fuss and then she'll scold. It's tough when your big sister is also your mom.

I trudge up the road back to the palace, my feet squishing with every step.

And then an icy rain begins, pelting my face.

By the time I reach the palace courtyard by the front door, my feet are numb, my calves are screaming from the steep uphill climb, and my face hurts. I peel off my muddy shoes and socks before entering the great hall, where a servant, an older man named Pierre, immediately appears to assist me. I explain about the car, and he assures me it'll be taken care of right away. No questions asked, thank goodness. Then he takes my wet hat, coat, shoes, and socks to be laundered, stopping to talk to a guard about the car.

Welp, looks like that will be getting back to Michael sooner rather than later. The other guards are like brothers to him. In hindsight, walking uphill in the freezing rain wasn't my smartest move—I should've called for a ride—but I'm just emotional enough not to be thinking clearly.

Pierre stops and turns to me. "Would you like a maid to assist you in returning to your room, Miss Chloe?"

"No, thank you."

He bows his head, turns, and leaves. He's kind enough

not to say a word about my appearance. I must look like a stray dog and feel as low.

I'm halfway upstairs when I hear baby Henry's cry down below. Sara must be on her way back to her room. I can't let her see me like this. I'm too exhausted to deal with any more drama today.

I race upstairs, my tight calves protesting the movement. The sound of Henry fussing gets closer and closer. I'll never make it to my room at the end of the long hallway before she spots me. I try the first door on my right. Locked. Second door. *Yes!*

I dash inside, quietly shut the door behind me, and turn, my lips parting in surprise. A half-dressed Rourke is standing there. The men in the Rourke family could've been stamped from the same mold. Who leaves their door unlocked while they're getting dressed?

My gaze lifts from his broad chest to his gorgeous face with sparkling blue eyes, sharp cheekbones, and a neatly trimmed beard. It's not just any Rourke. It's the one I spotted across the ballroom, drawn in by his wide smile. He looked like a good time waiting to happen—my complete opposite— and I longed to see what that would feel like. I was right too. When I asked Sara about him, she said he's known to love to party. I don't even enjoy the party scene. What is it about him? I missed my chance to meet him at the ball, after my misguided attempt to make amends with Michael that night (he was on guard duty and brushed me off), and now here he is. Half naked.

His fingers are still on the center button of an open white dress shirt exposing six-pack abs. I'm not looking at his navy blue boxer-briefs. Heat floods my cheeks, and my mouth goes dry. I peeked.

His deep voice is laced with good humor. "Uh, hi. Are ya okay there?"

2

____

Brendan

Chloe, the beautiful redhead who disappeared from the ball before I could ask her to dance, just burst into my bedroom. *Merry Christmas to me!* I asked the queen—the source of all family info—about Chloe after I saw her at the ball a few days ago. I wanted to be sure we weren't related because—lust at first sight. You never know at these royal functions who's family. I haven't seen her since, until she burst into my room.

She crosses her arms, hugging herself tightly, and shivers. A protective instinct I never knew I had takes over. I step closer and then remember I'm not wearing pants.

I hold up a finger. "Just a minute. Lemme get dressed and I'll help you." I grab my navy blue dress pants from where I left them on the bed and pull them on. "I'm Brendan."

She nods. "S-sorry, I didn't mean to intrude." Her teeth are chattering. "I'm C-Chloe."

I retrieve my leather jacket from the closet and wrap it around her shoulders. She's so petite it looks like a dress on her. "What happened? Were you in some kind of accident?" Her red hair hangs in wet frizzy clumps over her shoulders, her pink cardigan and matching tank top are soaked around the neck, her jeans are soaked through and streaked with mud and grass stains, and she's barefoot.

She shivers again and pulls the jacket closed. "It's a l-long story. Can we just say I got c-caught in the freezing rain?" Her voice is high and reedy.

A primitive alarm sounds in my brain. *Woman in distress. Must rescue.*

"Sure, okay," I say soothingly. I'm thinking about the best way to get her warm quick when she stiffens, listening carefully to voices in the hall. She puts a finger to her lips, asking me to be quiet. I hear a baby crying and what is most likely the baby's parents talking, but I can't make out who it is or what they're saying. There's a couple of babies and a toddler (who can still wail like a baby when she wants to) staying at the palace.

After they pass, she relaxes. "My sister and her family. She always goes by my room on her way up to hers."

"And you don't want to see her?"

"I don't want her to see me like this." Her voice chokes, and my chest tightens. Something happened to her, and all I want to do is make it better. "I just can't deal with any more drama today, you know?"

"Yeah."

"She's my big sister, but she raised me, so she's like my mom. She'll make a big deal."

What happened to her parents?

She takes off my jacket and hands it back. "Thanks. I'm going to get changed. I'm at the end of the hall."

"Sure you don't need some help?"

"I'm fine." She opens the door, peeks out, and quickly shuts it. "She's knocking on my door."

"Do you want me to tell her you went somewhere?"

She pulls her phone from her back jeans pocket. "I'll text her I'm studying in the library." She stares at her phone for a long moment, seeming to be reading a text, bites her lower lip, and texts rapidly.

Her expression caves, her teeth chattering again. I put my

jacket back around her shoulders and glimpse a text over her shoulder. *I need to not see you for a while, okay?*

I step away. That doesn't sound like something an older sister would say. It sounds like a guy cutting her loose.

After a few moments, she lets out a shuddering breath and lifts her head. "All s-set." Then she just stands there, clutching my jacket around her, looking lost.

"Go take a hot shower in my bathroom. You're gonna catch a chill." I head for my dresser and pull out a long-sleeved cotton shirt and jogging pants. I jerk my chin for her to follow. "Come on. I've got a warm change of clothes for you."

I turn the water on, hoping she follows. I really don't think she should wait any longer to warm up. Besides, I want to talk to her to make sure she's okay and see if there's anything I can do to help.

"Thanks," she says softly, stepping into the bathroom. She left my jacket behind, and she looks so small and vulnerable in her soaking wet state, shivering, her expression strained. I just want to scoop her up and battle the world back so nothing bothers her again. I'm not usually so heroic, but something about her brings that out in me.

"I'll go," I say, realizing I'm keeping her from the shower.

While Chloe showers, I finish getting dressed. Christmas dinner is in the formal dining room, which means you have to wear a blazer, dress shirt, and dress pants. I draw the line at a tie. Ties and I don't get along. It always feels like I'm one step away from a noose.

I take a seat on the gray sofa in the sitting room of my suite, prop my feet up on the coffee table, and pull out my phone. A while later, I hear the hair dryer—this place comes fully stocked for guests—and realize she's almost ready. I try to think of how to get her talking. It belatedly occurs to me she could have cuts that need attention. It looks like she fell. Did she get thrown from a car? A motorcycle? A bike? Those are very different levels of injury. And what happened to her shoes?

I hear the bathroom door open, and a few moments later

she appears in front of me. She's drowning in my clothes, even with the shirtsleeves rolled up and the jogging pants rolled at the ankles. It's comical but also damn cute.

She holds out her arms and smiles. My heart thumps harder. She's beautiful when she smiles. It lights up her face. "I know I look ridiculous, but I feel so much better, thanks."

"No problem. You wanna tell me what happened? Are you hurt anywhere?"

Her smile drops. "I'll survive."

I gesture to the sofa. "Have a seat."

"I should go."

I stand. "You sure you're okay?"

She raises her palms, the long sleeves hanging low under her arms like angel wings. She looks like an angel too. Her red hair falls in a soft wave to her shoulders, her green eyes gleam with intelligence, her features delicate—fine cheekbones, thin nose, a bow in her top lip. A sharp pang of lust hits. *Not now.* I need to know if she's okay.

"Chloe?"

She presses her lips tightly together. "Truth?"

"Absofuckinglutely."

Her lips twitch. "I accidentally got into a relationship with a friend."

"Hate when that happens." I have some experience in this area. Women are always falling for me after I tell them I'm not looking for serious. It's like I'm a challenge or something.

"Yeah," she says softly. "He doesn't want to see me anymore, even though I tried to make amends. I made sugar cookies. It's stupid." She looks away, her lips pinched tightly together. I have the urge to pull her into my arms, and then, once she's okay, I want to punch the guy who hurt her. She took the time to make sugar cookies. Geez, he could've at least showed some appreciation. I never had a woman bake anything for me. That takes real effort. I clench my jaw.

She continues. "Turns out we were never really friends." She blinks rapidly, crosses her arms, and stares at my chest. "It's just hard because this is my home when I'm not at college, and he was my only friend here."

And then the one thing I never thought I'd say to a woman I'm attracted to pops out of my mouth. "I'll be your friend while you're here." *What am I doing? Putting myself in the friend zone!*

Her brows lift over wide green eyes. "Oh, thanks. Are you here a lot?"

"I'm one of the Brooklyn Rourkes." *The riffraff.* That's what some of the older generation calls us since my dad abdicated the throne to marry my mom, a commoner. He was banished for it. "We recently reunited with the Villroy Rourkes, so it looks like I'll probably be here for holidays and family stuff."

"My sister married Adrian Rourke."

I know. The queen gave me the scoop. "Cool. That's my cousin."

It hits me like a smack upside the head. Forget lust at first sight. With our family connection, a casual hookup is out. There'd be too much potential fallout and awkward future encounters. *Dammit.* I've learned to be careful where women are concerned, making sure they don't expect anything more than casual from me. Obviously, that wouldn't work with someone connected to my family. Never mix family and flings. Or something like that.

Any misstep on my part will immediately fire through the family network. And, while the Villroy and Brooklyn Rourkes are on speaking terms right now, it's still new. You can't just undo decades of banishment with a few visits. I'm certainly not going to be the reason my dad loses his kingdom for a second time. It means a lot to him to be welcome in his ancestral land.

Guess the friend zone was a smart move. Ah, hell.

She wiggles her fingers. "Bye. I'll get your clothes back to you after they're cleaned."

"You don't have to do that."

"I won't. A servant will." She crinkles her nose. "Isn't it strange to have servants?"

"I wouldn't object to a full-time chef back home."

"Right?" She smiles and I smile back, our gazes locking for a charged moment before she looks away. Attraction is definitely not one-sided. "I'll just grab my clothes from the bathroom. I wrapped them in a towel to minimize the mess."

"I'll get them."

"No, I got it."

She turns and walks away. My jogging pants slip past her hips, and she clutches them with one hand. My shirt hangs past her ass, so I didn't get a peek at anything interesting. *Nope, not going there.* I tear my gaze away, telling myself it's for the best. Chloe is my friend. A woman friend. Now that's a first.

I'm sitting in the formal dining room for Christmas dinner and can't help but notice Chloe isn't here. I hope she's okay. We're having drinks to start, a dry champagne. King Gabriel sits at the head of the table with his wife, Queen Anna, on one side and his mother, the former queen, on his other side. It's pretty old-school traditional here, though from what I can tell, the king and queen rule together as equals. Their two-year-old daughter, Mila, sits on my dad's lap, talking in excited tones to him. Something about her secret fairy garden.

I purposely sat at the far end of the table, where there were still empty seats, hoping Chloe would sit near me. I glance across the table where Chloe's sister, Sara, sits with Adrian and their baby, Henry. I make a funny face at Henry when he notices me, widening my eyes and sticking my tongue out. He stares unblinking back, his eyes wide as saucers, before he gets distracted by Adrian passing him over to Sara. Chloe wouldn't miss Christmas dinner, would she?

Christmas is a big deal in my family. It's the only time everyone gets off work and can be together for a good time. Though I see plenty of my five brothers at work since we co-own Byrne Construction (my uncle's company before he retired) and the new company we formed under it, Rourke Management, for real estate development. My job is to scout out new properties ripe for development in Brooklyn. So far, I landed us a closed elementary school that we converted successfully to commercial office space, and our current project, an old marine rope factory by the waterfront that we're converting to lofts for design and artist tenants. I'm always on the lookout for the next project. I've got my eye on some low-level warehouses by the waterfront for possible residential space.

"Did Santa bring you everything you dreamed of?" my younger brother, Garrett, asks, interrupting my thoughts. We call him Beast on account of his overly muscled body. The dude lifts weights way beyond what's necessary. His barbells take up half his bedroom in our apartment. What's he going for? Hulk status?

I lean close, keeping my voice low. "Ya know, I think he might've. I caught up with the pretty redhead from the ball earlier." *Not that I'm going to do anything about it.*

He snorts. "Any woman can be fiery. Redhead, blonde, brunette." I always say I like redheads because they're more fiery. Though, I have to admit, Chloe seems more thoughtful than fiery.

I shrug one shoulder. "What can I say? I have a type."

"I love 'em all." He grins, his blue-green eyes twinkling with amusement. He's the only one of us who inherited my dad's blue-green eyes, which match the color of the sea here. Supposedly, it's the sign of the true leader of Villroy. Not that the youngest son of the formerly exiled family would ever be king. I think Garrett would be, let's see…twelfth in line for the throne. After King Gabriel, there's my cousins—four princes and two princesses—then there's our family with five brothers ahead of Garrett. Or, wait, maybe King Gabriel's little girl fits in there somewhere too. Garrett could be thirteenth in line. Lucky thirteen.

I chuckle. "Love 'em all, sow your wild oats. That sounds about right for twenty-four."

He shakes his head, smiling. "I just haven't met the One yet, ya know? She's out there somewhere."

I stifle a laugh. Underneath his tough-looking exterior, he's such a softie. *The One.* Like there's only one woman out there for you. Total BS. He should enjoy this time in his life when women close to his age aren't looking for long-term commitment so much. The women I've been meeting, closer to my age (twenty-six), it's definitely on their minds. Okay, there's a very specific reason for my new caution—Mallory. A couple of months back—after just three weeks of hooking up on Saturday nights—she says, "Where's this going, Bren? I deserve to know." I shouldn't have spent the night. That gave her the wrong idea. I'd told her up front I wasn't looking for serious. The worst part is, she cried when I ended it. Like bawled. And then she threw a pointy stiletto at my head. I ducked just in time. Not gonna lie, I felt like absolute shit about it. I don't want any woman crying over me. Which is why I'm being more careful now.

Don't get me wrong. Commitment is great for some guys. Like my older brothers—Dylan, married with a baby on the way in a couple of weeks; Sean, getting married soon on Valentine's Day (I know, barf); Jack's wedding is in June; and Connor just recently got engaged, no wedding date yet. Not to mention my parents.

I glance over as my dad clinks his champagne glass against my mom's. They smile, gazing into each other's eyes. He gave up everything to marry her, a commoner from Brooklyn, New York. It was hard on him, being exiled from his kingdom with nothing. No allowance, not even a small cushion to get him started. All so he could be with "the best woman in the world." His oft-repeated words. So I know for *some* guys the whole love and commitment thing works. And maybe one day when I'm too old to be on the prowl—forty or so—I'll settle down. But not now.

I glance at the dining room door when it opens, a rush of anticipation going through me. Nope, not her, just a servant in the uniform of white button-down shirt and black pants. The guy walks over for a word with the king and queen. Next he stops to talk to Chloe's sister, who stands, murmuring something to her husband, and leaves with the baby in her arms. *Is something wrong with Chloe?* Maybe she's in worse shape than I thought. She seemed okay when she left my room. I should've made sure.

I'm dying of curiosity, but I know it's not my place to butt in. Sara's on it. Another round of champagne is brought out and the conversation gets louder. My dad walks around the table to chat with everyone, with Mila in his arms. He's trying to keep her entertained while we wait for the meal to start. Usually it takes a while to get through a formal dinner with all the courses, and I think the queen wants to wait for everyone to arrive before we begin.

A short while later, a soft voice says, "Sorry I'm late, everybody."

It's her. Adrenaline fires through me, every nerve ending on alert. Her pink cheeks stand out against her creamy skin and red hair. She's holding her infant nephew cradled against her chest. My own chest aches at the sight. She just looks so natural and loving with a baby in her arms. Like a beautiful angel.

Get real, Bren. Cut the angel crap.

The irony is that my parents used to call me a little devil because I was mischievous as a kid. I've always liked to have fun. The angel and the devil. Ha! Not meant for the long term, but definitely worth a tangle or two. If only she weren't connected to the Rourke clan, I could act on it.

Why in the world did I volunteer to be her friend? This is too much to ask any red-blooded man.

I catch her eye. "Merry Christmas, Chloe."

She smiles warmly. "You too." She hands her nephew back to her sister and takes the seat across from me, unfolding her cloth napkin, looking self-conscious. She's wearing a white cardigan over a red dress that clings to her petite curves. My gut tightens. It's nothing blatantly sexy, the dress covers her up to her neck, but I can see her collarbones, the dip between them so feminine and tempting to trace and kiss and taste. *Whoa, whoa, whoa, back it up.*

I blink and turn away, realizing I'm staring. Probably with a hungry look on my face too. I'm usually much more subtle.

I glance over at Beast and he smirks. *Busted.* I've got to play it cool.

A few moments later, the first course arrives—oysters with

caviar. Aren't oysters an aphrodisiac? Not that I need one in my current state. I can't stop stealing glances at her. She speaks quietly to Sara and Adrian mostly. Her movements are graceful, her voice soft. Is she shy? She didn't seem shy earlier. She's definitely not upset. Not happy exactly, more like neutral. Serious.

A couple of servants circulate, offering wine, which she declines. I do too, being more of a beer drinker.

I focus back on my food. We always eat well here with lots of seafood since Villroy is an island and their fishing industry has sustained them for centuries. More recently the fishing industry has been used for the high-end cosmetics they use at their day spa. They also run a casino, which my brothers and I plan to enjoy tomorrow before heading home the next morning on the royal jet. Finally, it pays to be born a prince. I like to drop that into conversation when I pick up women. They never believe me at first, but they always *want* to believe. Now I can prove it by showing them my picture at my oldest brother Dylan's wedding on Villroy. Women go crazy in excitement when they see that, inevitably asking to visit the palace.

I catch her looking at me. Her lashes flutter down and she turns back to her sister. She was checking me out. I straighten my shoulders, my chest puffing out. But then I remember her vulnerable state earlier. I need to be her heroic protector friend. If denying my natural urges isn't heroic, then I don't know what is. Someone give me a medal.

The courses arrive one after the other—lobster, stuffed goose, mashed potatoes (also with lobster), Brussel sprouts, and some kind of vegetable I don't recognize. I join in the conversation, joking around with my brothers and occasionally lowering my voice when my dad sends me a pointed look meant to remind me of my manners. I can get loud sometimes. My dad is a stickler for manners because of his strict royal upbringing. Even through all that, my attention returns to Chloe again and again. Every time I catch her eye, she looks away. I know she's sneaking looks at me too. I can feel it.

After a delicious dessert called a Noel log, we're invited back to the parlor for brandy by the fire. I like the parlor, it's the most comfortable room in the palace with its leather sofas and club chairs, but first I need to know if Chloe's going to be there. I really do want to check in with her.

She darts out the dining room door before anyone else, and I follow her.

"Hey, Chloe, are ya heading to the parlor for drinks?"

She turns and shakes her head. "I don't drink."

"Why not?"

"I'm not twenty-one yet."

Didn't I say she was like an angel? I've heard drinking is real popular with the college crowd.

I close the distance, my lips curving into a small smile. "This is Villroy. Legal age to drink is eighteen."

She crinkles her adorable nose. "No, thanks."

"Well, you don't have to drink. Everyone's just gonna be hanging out. Come on, it'll be fun."

Her green eyes search mine. "Are you, like, hitting on me?"

Man, I suck at this friend thing.

Heat creeps up my neck. "No. What? No. Why would you say that?" I gesture down the hall. "I was just wondering if you were joining us."

She studies me for a long moment.

Did I protest too much?

"Okay," she says. "I'm going back to my room now."

"Why?"

"To read medical journals."

My eyes widen in surprise. I thought she was in college. She's already reading medical journals? Isn't that what doctors do?

I stare at her. "Are you going to be a doctor?"

She nods. "I plan to be a medical researcher and cure cancer."

I gape for a moment. I can't help it. It's not just because it's such a noble cause. It's the way she says it, plainly, matter-of-factly. "Wow. Okay."

She lifts her chin. "It's important work."

"No question." I shove my hands in my pockets. "But did ya ever hear all work and no play makes for a dull brain?"

She scowls. "Did you just call me dull?"

I grin. "Not you, your brain. You have to take time off to keep your mind sharp."

More of my family spills into the hall, talking and laughing. I glance over my shoulder at them and turn back to her. "So maybe we could do something besides drinks in the parlor. Something fun." I want to spend time with her, whether or not it leads to anything more. She's just so different from the women I usually meet. And I want to hear her story, what really happened today that had her showing up in my room looking like she was tossed from a moving vehicle.

"Something fun," she echoes, her brows knitting as if she has to think hard about it. I almost want to laugh. Who thinks hard about having fun?

Her sister appears with baby Henry asleep on her shoulder. "Hi, Brendan." I met her at her wedding to my cousin, though somehow I missed Chloe at the time. Probably because that wedding was the first time in decades our family showed up on Villroy after my dad was banished. Tense times.

"Hey, Sara. Looks like your little guy conked out early." Henry's mouth hangs wide open.

"Aww," Chloe says, stroking his cheek and then kissing it. Something in the vicinity of my heart shifts.

Sara smiles at the baby and then gets serious as she lifts her gaze to Chloe. "I'm going to put him to bed. Me too. I'm still up at least three times a night with him. I just wanted to check in with you. Are you doing okay?" She sounds very motherly and concerned.

Chloe glances at me, looking embarrassed. "I'm fine." Her voice is tight.

"You sure?" Sara presses. "I don't mind if you want to come back to my room for a bit to study."

Chloe shakes her head. "No, you need your sleep. I'm okay."

"Really?" Sara asks.

Chloe exhales sharply. "I was just about to do something with Brendan."

Sara looks between us for a moment curiously before taking a step back. "Okay, then. I'll see you in the morning. Goodnight." She heads down the hall.

Chloe stares at the marble floor, her brows knit together in a scowl. Nothing like a big sister/mom to get your feathers ruffled, I guess.

I dip my head to meet her eyes and smile. "I'm all yours, party girl."

$$3$$

Chloe

It's so embarrassing the way Sara checks in on me over and over. I'm fine. And we had a long talk earlier, where I told her that. I'm grateful for what she's done for me, but I'm old enough where I need her more as a sister than a mom.

I meet Brendan's gaze. His brows lift over bright blue eyes —such a startling blue it's hard to look away—his expression expectant. I tear my gaze away from those hypnotizing eyes, but I can't quite look away from him completely. His dark brown hair is longish on top and tousled, probably soft to the touch. His hair combined with his neatly trimmed beard and devilish smile give him a rakish look. I got that rakish thing from my sister-in-law's historical romance books. I read one just to see what the fuss was about with all her awards and bestseller status. And I bet Brendan's a rake, always on the lookout for his next conquest.

Before this goes any further, I inform him, "I'm not looking for a hookup. Just so we're clear."

His lips twitch. "That would be like kissing my cousin. So wrong."

I stiffen. I could've sworn he was checking me out earlier at dinner. I look away, my cheeks heating. I feel like a total wiener, assuming he was into me. He must've been looking at me at dinner because I kept checking *him* out. I didn't want to. He's just, well, any woman with a pulse would notice how sexy and gorgeous he is, even more so than all the other Rourke men because his eyes sparkle and he's always ready to smile. He looks like a good time in *every* way. My blush spreads to my neck at the thought. I'm not going there.

He leans down to my ear, his breath fanning hot over my skin, making a shiver rush down my spine as he whispers, "Let's be friends." Only it sounds like *let's hook up.*

But that's just my mind playing tricks on me. The words are so at odds with my body's reaction to him I'm thrown off-kilter.

He draws back, a small smirk on his face and a knowing look in his eyes. "Or you could always hang with your big sister. She seems pretty concerned about you."

That does it. I don't need my sister/mom hovering over me, making sure I'm okay. And just to prove it, I'm not going directly back to my room to study. I'm going to do exactly what I said I would. Hang with this guy, who sees me as a platonic friend. Or cousin. Great. Fine. It. Will. Be. Fun.

"Come on." I jerk my head for him to follow. I step past the dining room, heading for the tower room down the hall. I can hear people still talking in the dining room, slow to leave. Eventually they'll all be in the parlor, but I'm not in the mood for a crowd.

Halfway to the tower room, I slow my step. Michael is walking toward us, his short blond hair and gray T-shirt damp with sweat. He was probably working out in the gym downstairs.

"Where are you taking me?" Brendan asks, oblivious to the upcoming confrontation.

I can't seem to find my voice. Michael's gaze bounces from me to Brendan and back, his brows drawing down.

"Earth to…" Brendan trails off as Michael stops in front of me.

A muscle works in Michael's jaw. "Thank you for the cookies."

"You're welcome."

He gets in Brendan's face. They're about the same height and build—six feet of broad-shouldered muscle—but Michael is trained to disarm, disable, and destroy if necessary. My heart's in my throat. Brendan holds his ground.

Michael grinds out between his teeth, "Touch her and die." He straightens and salutes Brendan. "Joking. It's my duty and an honor to protect the Rourkes." He drops his hand and marches off like a soldier. It's funny but not.

I resume walking toward the tower room, not sure what to say after that.

"So that wasn't disturbing at all," Brendan says under his breath.

I give him a sideways look. "He's a palace guard. My ex."

"So you brought a trained assassin cookies?"

"You'd want to stay on his good side too, wouldn't you?"

He stops, suddenly serious. "Has he threatened you? Would he hurt you?"

"No. The royal family made him captain of the guards. If they trust him, why wouldn't I?"

He shakes his head. "I don't trust him farther than I can throw him." He grins, his eyes sparkling devilishly. "You, on the other hand, I could trust really, really far. You're so tiny." He mimes throwing me a distance like a football, letting out a long whistle as I presumably soar through the air.

I huff and continue on to the tower room. "I'm not tiny. I'm petite."

"I so want to toss you through the air—to a soft landing place, of course—but your ex would kill me if I touched you, so *that's out*." He shakes his head like he's annoyed, a smile tugging at his lips.

"Throwing me was never a possibility, you nut." I don't think Brendan is ever serious. I mean, Michael basically just threatened him and he took it in stride. I'm a little nervous about the whole thing. Not for me, for Brendan. The poor guy is just being friendly. He doesn't even think of me like that.

I head to the back of the tower room and use both hands to pull open a wooden bookcase that doubles as a door to a secret passageway.

Brendan's eyes go wide, and then he gives me a warm appreciative smile. "Very cool."

I smile back. It almost feels like he thinks I'm very cool too. Something I've never been accused of. I slip inside and walk down a sloped stone passageway with low ceilings. The light is dim, just what's filtering in through the open doorway.

Brendan pulls his phone out of his dark blue blazer and turns on the flashlight. I watch his expression as he takes in the hallway. Sara showed me this place. It used to be an escape route to the side exit of the palace, a form of defense, but now it's a storage area.

"What are these?" he asks, shining a light on a stone sculpture. "Cupids?"

"They're cherubs." The hallway is filled with them, mostly hung on the wall, some of them leaning against it. "They were part of an older section of the palace that was removed after the great fire."

"This is so cool."

I follow him as he shines his light on more cherubs, some of them broken but still cute, as we move farther down the hall. A sense of peace comes over me. It's fun to show off a part of the palace few know about, and I love these cherubs with their sweet chubby faces just waiting for visitors to admire them once again.

Brendan turns to me, lowering his phone so the light's not in my eyes. "I had no idea any of this was here. Did your ex show you this?"

I deflate. "No, my sister. Can we not talk about my ex? It's kind of a touchy situation."

He curls his lip in a snarly face and growls, "Touch her and die." Then in his regular voice, "Got it. Psycho ex."

"He's just a little peeved because I turned down his proposal."

"Oh, shit. He proposed? That's major. I thought it was more of a casual thing. No wonder he got in my face."

"Well, it was three months ago."

He cocks his head. "And how long were you accidentally in a relationship with him?"

I cringe, hearing my own words come back to me. "Okay, here's what you have to understand. It was off and on over the course of eleven months or so, only when I was here on school breaks."

"Eleven months! That's an awfully long time for casual." He grins. "It's nice to meet someone worse at relationships than I am."

I tense, feeling defensive. "I was clear from the start I didn't have space in my life for a relationship. I'm very focused on my studies. I'm in my second year at Columbia, one more to go, and then I'm heading to medical school. After that, there's more training with a residency and a fellowship. I've got a long haul ahead of me." I push my palm out. "I mean *long* haul. After I become a cancer researcher, then I'll look for someone to settle down with."

He puts a hand on my arm. "Chloe, you don't have to explain yourself to me. I get it."

I calm down. "Oh. Thanks."

"Also, what are you, a genius? Graduating Columbia in three years instead of four? And that's a top school. Even the valedictorian of my high school was rejected from Columbia."

I lift one shoulder in a small shrug. "I'm just a hard worker."

"Right. So-o-o, do you know any more secret passageways?"

"Just one more. It leads to the dungeon."

"Seriously? Let's go see that."

I shake my head. "It's gross. There's spiders and I don't even know what else crawling around down there, and it smells like creepy mold."

He laughs. "Never heard of creepy mold."

"You especially don't want to go there at night. It's cold and dark." I cross my arms, fighting a shiver at the thought. "I think there's bats too."

He leans against the wall, crossing his arms over his chest. "You want to hang here for a while?"

"Yeah. Can I borrow your light? I left my phone in my room."

"Sure, but first I want something from you."

I still, suddenly wary.

He laughs. "You look like I'm about to ask for your first-born." He reaches out and nudges my shoulder. "I just wanted to know how you ended up soaking wet, dirty, and shivering in my room earlier."

I lean against the wall next to him. Something about the intimate space makes it easier to share. So I tell him the whole ridiculous story—from cookies to planter to runaway car.

He turns to me. "You cared that much about keeping the friendship?"

"I felt bad that I hurt him."

"That's damn heroic what you did."

"Nah."

"Yeah," he insists.

I exhale sharply. "Turns out friends with benefits isn't really a thing. The friend part is fake."

He's quiet for a moment, seeming to consider this, before finally saying, "You're right. No guy wants to go back to being friends once they cross the line."

I straighten and hold out my palm for his phone. "Lesson learned."

He gives it to me, his eyes intent on mine. "You have a big heart."

"I do?" I feel hopeful for a moment, but then I realize he doesn't know me well enough to see the real me, on the inside. Broken.

"Hell yeah. You put in real time and effort making those cookies and getting them over there. You suffered to make amends. Only someone with a big heart would do all that. Most people would just walk away."

"Maybe I *should* have just walked away."

He chucks me under the chin. "Hey, nothing wrong with having a big heart. That's probably what makes you want to cure cancer. You want to give back to the world."

A warmth spreads through me. He's right about one thing —it's so important to me to give back. "Thanks."

He inclines his head.

I turn away, using the light on his phone to go farther down the passageway, checking out cherubs on my way to my favorite sculpture of a pair of cherubs. I stop to admire them, forever frozen on either side of a stone buttress. They look like they're peeking at each other. So close, yet so far.

I cross to him and hand back his phone. "Thanks. I'm ready to go." I lead the way out.

"That's enough fun, huh?" he says from behind me.

I can hear the smile in his voice. He's teasing me that I never have fun. "I'll have you know I make time for fun with my roommate, Lindsey, every weekend and after finals."

"Oh, yeah? What do you do?"

"Movie night, beauty night, sometimes we hit up the planetarium."

"Do you call that last one nerd night?"

I press my lips together. I've heard that taunt plenty in my life. I'm not a nerd. I'm a serious student. There's a difference.

I wait until we're back in the tower room, after closing the bookcase door securely behind us, to respond, "I prefer my friends to be less insulting."

He holds up his palms. "I meant nerd in the cool genius way. I do think what you're aiming for is noble." He gestures toward me. "Like a higher calling."

I breathe deep, pride making me stand straighter. "Thank you."

"What do you do on beauty night?" He glances at my nails. "You don't seem to paint anything or wear much makeup."

I actually am wearing makeup, but it's subtle. It's kinda flattering that he thinks I just naturally look like this. "This last beauty night after finals I dyed my hair red. She dyed hers purple."

He closes his eyes. "No." He sounds terribly despondent.

"What?"

He opens his eyes. "You're not a real redhead?"

"No, I'm blond like Sara. Why is that a big deal?"

He waves that away. "Nothing, don't worry about it. Hey, I brought my laptop. You want to watch the latest *Fast and the Furious* movie?"

"Is that the long series of movies about car chases?"

"Yeah, it's awesome. A new one just came out."

I tap my chin. "Hmm, I'm afraid I'll be totally lost since I didn't see all the car chases that came before it."

He gives a lock of my hair a tug. "Smart. We'll get started on the first one."

I get lost for a moment in his sparkling blue eyes. I bet his life is nonstop good times. What an easy life he must've had growing up, surrounded by people who love him, all that good humor and cheer. He probably never had a lonely moment in his entire life. Ever. The contrast with my own life is almost laughable. Sara and I had each other and that's it. I had long lonely spells while she was at work. Maybe that's why I poured myself into my schoolwork. I have to admit, no matter how good you are at science, it doesn't give you the warm feeling that just standing near Brendan and his family does.

No use wishing for what I never had. Education is my springboard to a better life, both for financial security and to make a difference in the world. Growing up, my sister and I barely scraped by. I'm seriously torn between the fun he promises and my need to get back to work. "I dunno, Brendan. This sounds like it could take a while."

"Nah. Couple of hours, and then you can catch up on the other movies on your own time."

I consider another angle. Watching a movie on his laptop means we'll be in close proximity. I can't deny I'm drawn to him. Then again, he said kissing me would be like kissing his cousin. Okay, the smart thing to do is to keep him at a safe distance. That way there's no risk of me acting impulsively on completely natural biological urges.

"You'll like it, I promise," he says in a coaxing voice. "It's universally appealing, even to future doctors. What's your last name?"

"Travers."

"Even for you, Dr. Travers."

I bite back a smile. I've been waiting my whole life for someone to call me Dr. Travers. I *love* the sound of it. *Dr. Chloe Travers.*

Chloe Travers, MD.

Dr. Travers, we need your opinion on this atypical cell formation.

I shrug. "Okay."

He grins and leads the way to his room. We settle on an overstuffed gray sofa in the sitting room to watch the movie on his laptop set up on the coffee table. He slouches down on the sofa, his gaze glued to the movie. Guess I don't have to worry about the close proximity thing. It's clear he's more interested in a movie he's already seen than in me. No problem. I get comfortable and force myself to keep my eyes on the screen, pretending I'm alone, ignoring the heat of his body and his sexy woodsy scent. *Focus on the car chases and swaggering men.*

Next thing I know, I startle awake, wiping the drool from my mouth. Oh my God. I fell asleep, and my head is resting on his shoulder.

I slowly straighten and look up at him.

He smiles, his blue eyes warm on mine. "What's your professional opinion of the movie, Dr. Travers?"

I smile widely, my chest warming at his turn of phrase. "I liked it."

"Which part?"

I think back to the early part of the movie before I fell asleep. "The hot swaggering guy part."

"Uh-huh. Any particular one?"

I stare at the laptop screen, trying to remember the name of the actor. It's on a screensaver of shooting stars. How long was I sleeping? Did he just sit here letting me sleep on his shoulder for hours? That was so nice of him.

"Vin Diesel?" he prompts. "You dig the baldies?"

I laugh and meet his eyes sparkling down at me. My gaze drops to his sensual lips that always seem to want to smile.

Suddenly I feel this pull, like I want to get closer. Chemistry is a powerful thing.

"Chloe." His voice sounds rough.

I lick my lips. "All the guys were hot." But I mean him.

I should leave, but I can't seem to move.

He stands and offers me a hand. I get off the sofa on my own, not trusting myself to touch him. I feel close to him for some reason. Silly. Just because I fell asleep on him and he let me for…I don't even know how long.

I study him for a moment, and he studies me right back as we stand facing each other in front of the sofa. It's like we're trying to figure out next steps. Are we really friends? If so, we could hang out tomorrow too. I don't know if I should mention it.

He hitches a thumb toward the door. "You want me to walk you back to your room?"

"I'm just down the hall. I think I can make it."

He laughs.

He's so good natured. Some people are put off by my dry humor. "Goodnight, Brendan. Thanks for the movie."

"No problem." One corner of his mouth tilts up and a dimple appears in his scruffy cheek. It's immensely appealing. I tell myself it's just a dent and it's not like he can help it. "Thanks for showing me your secret passageway." He closes his eyes for a moment. "And I didn't mean that as dirty as it sounded. Think you'll watch more of the *Fast and the Furious* movies?"

"No."

His brows lift over eyes sparkling with good humor. "I'll have to report you to the Vin Diesel fan club."

I giggle and then immediately smother it. So not like me to giggle. I leave with a wiggle of my fingers over my shoulder at him.

By the time I reach my room again, I'm smiling, which just goes to show I do know how to have fun.

4

—————

Brendan

Today's my last day on Villroy, and I'm making the most of it, playing poker at the casino with my brothers and cousins in a private room. Does it get any better than this? Free drinks, good company, and I'm up by a couple of hundred euros. There's two games going on right now, mixing it up between Villroy and Brooklyn folk. Adrian is the one to watch at my table, a true card shark. He doesn't need the money. He owns this place and it's immensely successful, but he plays each hand like his life depends on winning it.

I have the feeling Adrian's going to surprise us with a full house. He's surprised us twice already. I just got lucky with my last hand, and I know it. My mind keeps drifting back to Chloe. I guess some part of me was hoping for more fun with her. I'm leaving tomorrow morning. She avoided family meals and didn't join us at the casino either. Adrian told me earlier that she's staying on Villroy for three weeks before returning to college. It's not like she'd want to see me back home once school is back in session, so now is the time for fun. I don't know why I keep thinking of her. It's just—

Her smile.

It felt like such a victory to see her smile, especially once I realized what a serious person she is, so focused on her studies. *I did that.*

Beast elbows me in the ribs. "Your redhead is here."

My head jerks up. She just walked in with her sister. She looks like a young college student, wearing a green cardigan over a matching tank top with jeans and short black suede boots. Duh, she is a young college student. She's not for me. She's too serious, too driven, too…doctor-y.

Family connection. Fallout. Awkwardness.

Psycho assassin ex. Death.

And then she bites her lower lip and gives me a tentative wave. It hits me like a gut punch.

I stand and throw my cards on the table facedown. "I fold."

A chorus of protests erupts.

"What?" I ask, my eyes glued to Chloe. She's checking out the room while talking to her sister.

"Seriously?" Beast asks.

"Lame, man!" one of my brothers barks. I can't bother to see who it is.

I'm already crossing the room, forcing myself to keep to a slow, even stride, so I don't look as eager as I feel. I catch her eye and smile. She smiles back and warmth spreads through me.

"Hey, Chloe," I say when I finally reach her. "Taking a break?"

"No, I'm studying anatomy as we speak," she deadpans.

"Anyone's in particular?" I look around and find a bald man circulating with drinks. I speak out of the side of my mouth. "The baldie, right?"

She giggles and slaps a hand over her mouth.

I grin. "Vin Diesel would be so jealous."

"I'm joining a game," Sara says to Chloe.

I realize I was rude. Her sister has been standing here the whole time. "Hi, Sara, good to see ya again."

"Sure, sure," she says with a smile in her voice before joining Adrian. She'll probably take my place in the game.

Chloe shakes her head. "She says you're my new boy toy."

"Ridiculous. I'm all man."

"Man toy doesn't rhyme."

"Hmm, how about Bam Man?"

She quirks a brow. "Really? As in slam, bam, thank you, ma'am? Not a compliment to you that you're an early finisher."

I straighten at the insult. "I'm not, trust me. Anyway, what's up?"

"Sara forced me out of my room."

"Did she drag you over by the hair?"

"She's very persistent."

"Okay, well, you're here. So are ya into poker?"

"Not really. I can play. Sara's awesome at it and we've played together lots of times. I just don't find it fun."

"Slots? There's roulette downstairs, craps, and—"

"I know, Brendan. I've been here many times."

I cock my head. "Right. So what do you like to do?"

"Mostly I hang here long enough to get Sara off my back and then go back to my room to study."

"Is that really what you want to do?" I lift my palms. "I mean, you've got a charming friend ready and willing to play with you."

She giggles and slaps a hand over her mouth again.

I pull her hand down. "Why do you hide a laugh, party girl?"

"I surprised myself with it. You're funny."

My chest puffs out. "Yeah, I know. So...what'll it be?"

She puts her hands on her hips, drops them, and then crosses her arms. "I don't know."

She looks so uncomfortable in the noisy space it occurs to me that someone who spends most of their time studying is used to library quiet. She'd never have survived growing up in the Rourke household—six rambunctious boys in a three-bedroom rowhouse. Luckily, my parents finished the basement into a rec room/extra bedroom to give us more room to spread out.

"You wanna go somewhere quieter?" I ask.

Her green eyes light up. "Yes."

"Let's go downstairs to the bar. It's not crowded. Adrian says more people visit the casino over New Year's Eve than Christmas. You could get something nonalcoholic."

"Sure, okay."

I lead the way. "Was it pretty quiet growing up with just one sister? I ask because I have five brothers and it was never, ever quiet."

"Actually, yes, but also because my parents died when I was six. I don't remember much of the time when it was the four of us."

No wonder she's so serious. Six is really young to lose your parents. "That must've been tough."

She walks a little faster. "Yeah. After that we lived with my uncle in Brooklyn, but then when I was nine, he left to make it big in Nashville as a country singer, so it's just been me and Sara ever since. She's seven years older and worked a lot to support us. Anyway, that's why I'm used to a lot of quiet time alone."

"I'm sorry. I didn't mean to bring up a painful subject."

She shrugs. "It's my life. No sense trying to rewrite history and wish for something different. I just had to make the best with what I was given."

True. I just feel so bad for her. No wonder Sara fusses over her. She practically raised her like a single mom. I feel bad for Sara too. The two of them got a bum deal.

"Let's talk about something else," she says as the bar comes into view. "Your family is very noisy. The Brooklyn Rourkes *and* the Villroy Rourkes. Is that genetic, or do you think it's a matter of survival, trying to be heard over the crowd so you get your fair share of resources?"

I bark out a laugh just as we enter the bar area. It's past nine p.m. and the place is practically empty, like I predicted, just the bartender and two young guys at the end of the bar. The guys check Chloe out, take in my glare, and go back to the boxing match on TV.

"Genetic," I say in answer to her noisy Rourke question. "But you snooze, you lose on food resources. The moment a tub of ice cream entered the house, it was gone within five minutes." I take a seat at the bar and she takes the one next to me. "I never felt like I had to fight to get anything else. I got my parents' fair share of attention easily just by being myself. They called me a mischievous little devil." I wink at her.

She gives me side-eye. "I could see that about you."

I grin and pound my chest with a fist. "Yup."

"What can I get you?" the bartender, an older man with thinning brown hair, asks.

I glance over at the selections on tap and order a Belgian ale.

"Do you have anything fruity?" Chloe asks.

"Sure do." The bartender hands her a drink menu.

I lean over to read it with her. There's a lot of funny-sounding cocktails playing off royalty and Villroy—royaltini, Villroy breeze, even a lobster snap.

"I can make anything without alcohol too," the bartender says. "We also have soda." He points it out on the back of the menu.

"Can you give me a few minutes to decide?" Chloe asks.

He inclines his head and moves farther down the bar, pouring my beer.

Chloe leans close to confide, "My sister says I used to be a devilish whirlwind when I was little, though I don't remember any of it."

"You, really?"

She nods. "She says I used to rip off my clothes and run all over the beach naked, destroy sandcastles that she and Princess Silvia helped me build, throw our lunch to the seabirds, and pull the legs off crabs." Princess Silvia is Adrian's twin, which means Chloe's been close with the Villroy Rourkes for a while.

"My kind of girl. So what made you come to Villroy when you were little?" Before the casino and spa, it wasn't exactly a destination.

"My dad was originally from France and had fond memories of summers on Villroy. I spent every summer here since I was a baby. Sara was close with Silvia and Adrian since they're all the same age. I was the crazy little sister they had to put up with."

So, basically, the royal family has known Chloe since she was born. And now my cousin is her brother-in-law. Yup, definitely have to be careful not to cross the line with this one. Talk about family fallout.

"What other devilish things did you do?" I ask.

She smiles and ducks her head. "Apparently, I swallowed a fish too, but that was accidental. I thought I could keep it alive in the spit in my mouth and bring it home to be my pet."

"Now that I've never done. I put my dad's credit card in the mailbox once. I wanted to see it slide down the slot. Boy, was he mad."

She shakes her head. "Kids, right?" She studies the menu again. "I've never had a drink in my life, but all this talk about my carefree days makes me want to try one." She meets my eyes with a small smile on her beautiful angelic face. "Be a little wild."

I stiffen, on full alert. Chloe can't get wild. She'll be way too tempting. Wild women are my bread and butter. I can't eat here! This is family territory.

"Bad idea," I say.

"Why?"

I shake my head, desperately hoping to rattle a good reason out of my panicking brain. "Because."

"Just one. And I can call for a ride back to the palace. Sensible and fun." She goes back to the menu, drawing her lower lip into her mouth as she studies it. My gut tightens. Something about those lips with the bow at the top and the fuller lower lip. *So sexy*. I tear my gaze away from temptation.

My beer arrives, and I take a long swallow. Feeling calmer, I channel my oldest brother's responsible-sounding voice. "Best to avoid alcohol since you don't have a tolerance. Drink responsibly." Wait. I think that's from a commercial encouraging people to drink, but in a responsible way.

She turns to me. "The Villroy breeze sounds refreshing with the strawberries. Is rum sweet?"

I open my mouth to say rum tastes like cough syrup and should be avoided at all costs, but it's too late.

She lifts a hand to the bartender. "I'll take the Villroy breeze, please. With alcohol."

I hang my head. This is terrible. Now she's going to get all loose and relaxed, exactly how I like my women. If she gets wild, I'm a goner.

She grabs my beer, takes a sip, and sticks her tongue out. "Blech."

"Right? Skip that. I bet your drink is bad too." I turn away and take another long swallow of beer. As soon as I'm done with this beer, I'm going back to the poker game. I'll drop her off with her sister and keep my distance for the rest of the night.

She elbows me in the ribs. "Don't let me do anything crazy or embarrassing."

I gulp. "Like what?"

"I don't know." She flutters a hand in the air. "Something."

She can't even imagine something wild. Excellent. Maybe the alcohol won't have any effect on her. She'll just giggle or something.

I relax and fill in the blanks of what wild could mean. It's funny because she'd never do any of it. "Like dance naked on a table?"

She smiles. "No. I don't dance."

Perfect. Now I can have fun with her.

I lower my voice so the bartender who's preparing her drink at the other end of the bar can't hear. "Do a striptease for the old guy behind the bar here?"

Her eyes widen. "Why does everything end with me naked?"

I lift my beer, hiding a smile. "You did have a fondness for being naked as a kid."

She shakes her head. "Right? I'm such a wuss now."

"You totally are."

"Hey!"

I chuckle quietly, and she shoots me a dark look. She's not used to teasing. "I'm just agreeing with you," I tell her.

A few minutes later, I watch as she takes her first tentative sip. "Mmm, it's delicious!"

The protector comes out in me. "Careful, sometimes the sweet stuff disguises the alcohol and you drink it too fast." I'm not sure if I'm protecting her or me.

She slurps again and presses her fingers to her forehead. "Brain freeze. Let's split some lobster nachos. I skipped dinner."

I straighten in my seat. "Chloe, never drink on an empty stomach."

"Yes, sir," she says sharply.

Did I come off too harsh? I'm the chill guy you party with. Man, this is fucked up.

I try for a friendly tone. "Sure, I can always go for nachos."

She places the order and turns back to me. "I like having a guy friend. It's like you're a natural repellant to any other guy who might approach." She inclines her head toward the two guys at the end of the bar. They're in their twenties, probably locals.

I clench my jaw. *Just what I always wanted to be—guy repellant.*

One beer and I'm out of here.

I guzzle down a healthy amount. I'm starting to feel it, actually, because it's my third beer of the night. I had a couple earlier at the poker game. Good thing we ordered nachos. I should slow down on this beer.

She pokes my chest. "Guess what?"

She's touching me.

I look over. "What?" Oh, shit. Her drink is nearly gone.

"I feel super happy." She gasps. "Is this what a buzz feels like?"

I stifle a laugh. "Yeah."

She laughs and drains her glass. "Fantastic work here, Mr. Bartender. Can you bring another?"

He inclines his head and gets to work.

"That's fine, but eat before you drink any more," I say. "Got it?" I sound like a total buzzkill. I *am* a total buzzkill. I just can't let this situation get out of hand.

"Bren-dan." She stretches out my name in a playful voice. "I'm fine."

"I say this as your good friend with experience in alcohol territory. You're small and you have no tolerance." *And now I sound like I have a stick up my ass.* I console myself that it's the protective instinct she brings out in me. I'm still a fun guy. Really.

"Small," she scoffs. "I pack a mighty punch." She punches my shoulder and it feels like a tap. That's not me playing tough. It's like she's never thrown a punch in her life.

I wince like it hurt, and she rubs my shoulder. "Sorry," she singsongs. "Now you'll have to admit I'm five feet three of pure power."

The bartender approaches with her drink, and I shake him off. "Can you bring it with the nachos?"

"Brendan Rourke!" she exclaims.

"Dr. Travers."

She sobers. "Am I acting embarrassing?"

"Just a little loud."

"Okay, you're the expert." She nods at the bartender to hold the drink.

I relax. "That's right. I'm the expert on Villroy breezes for virgin drinkers."

"Oh, I'm not a virgin."

Walked right into that one.

I shake my head as she leans close. I just know she's about to overshare. "Don't—"

She goes on in a loud stage whisper. "I lost it to Mike at biomedical engineering summer camp when I was sixteen. I had a full scholarship at Penn's special camp for science enthusiasts 'cuz that's how I roll."

My shoulders tense. *Was Mike another student or a teacher? And what is it with her and guys named Michael?* "And how old was Mike?"

"Sixteen."

I relax.

"He wasn't very good at it at first, but—"

"No need to—"

She holds up a finger. "By the end of the summer, he *finally* found the magic button." She pulls me by the shoulder to whisper loudly in my ear, "I'm being polite for mixed company. Of course, the correct anatomical term is…" She bursts out laughing, and I jerk back to save my hearing.

"I'm really feeling it now, Bren!"

I can't help but laugh. "I'm getting that."

She sighs happily. "I like having a guy friend. Now you can tell me the guy point of view. Why do guys think a woman sitting alone at the library studying wants to talk about what she's doing over the weekend?"

She looks perplexed. *Does she not realize how beautiful and sexy she is?*

She shakes my shoulder. "Come on, you're a guy. Tell me why they do that."

I blow out a breath. *How did I end up being the guy friend again?* This is hard work, not crossing the line. I keep it simple, stick to the facts. "You're a pretty girl—"

"Woman."

"You're a pretty woman who's sitting alone, so they think you're single. They're hoping to be with you."

She shakes her head. "But it's the library. Duh! Obviously I'm there to study."

"That's why they're asking you out for later. Most people go out on the weekends."

"Most people aren't aiming for Harvard Medical School. Besides, my physical needs were already met. What else do I need a guy for?"

"Nothing." I agree with her there. What else is there, unless you want to get into deep committed territory?

She smiles widely, and my heart thumps harder. She's irresistible when she's smiling. And when she's not.

Ah, hell. I need to get out of here. But I feel responsible for her now. I didn't think she'd get drunk just from one drink. Of course, I didn't know she'd skipped dinner either. I can't leave a drunk woman loose in the casino. She might do something she regrets later. As soon as she's done her second drink (and no more than that, I'm putting my foot down), and eats her fill of nachos, I'll see her safely back to her room. And that is that.

Hopefully, she'll get a hangover and decide it's not worth torturing a guy like this ever again.

5

Chloe

Brendan is being so-o-o gross. I'm glad I didn't grow up with brothers. He's got cheese string from the nachos caught on his chin beard. I'd tell him about it, but he doesn't need to look any hotter, thank you very much. I like having fruity alcohol drinks with him. I'm a wee bit tipsy, but it's okay. Brendan is being sensible enough for the both of us.

The nachos are delicious, and I devour more than my share. I take my time with my second drink, wanting it to last. No way I'm going for three drinks. Brendan said so. He's the expert. I also drank a big glass of water. I'll probably have to pee at three a.m.

"So what made you want to cure cancer?" he asks.

I chew and swallow. "It's the scourge of our existence, and I want to help humanity. The whole world." I wipe my mouth with the back of my hand. "Dedicating my life to it."

"Did someone close to you suffer from it?"

"No. My parents were hit by a drunk truck driver when they were walking on the sidewalk." I turn at his silence. Oh no, not that, anything but that. He's looking at me with sympathy in his eyes. I put my hand over his eyes.

He smiles and, dammit, he still looks gorgeous. "What don't you want me to see?"

"I don't wanna see you, Brendan-bo-bendan." I drop my hand and pull the cheese string out of his beard and hand it to him. He pops it in his mouth. "Eww, boys are gross."

"Men."

I laugh. "Men are gross."

"I'm very well trained. I always put the toilet seat down."

"Your mother raised you right."

"She did, but my dad is also a real stickler for manners and etiquette since he was raised here to be king. Seriously, though, what makes you so focused on being a cancer researcher? There's other ways to help humanity."

I go for the last nacho and hold it aloft for a moment, surprised he let me take it. "My high school had a science research course. I was matched up with a professional mentor involved in cancer research. It piqued my interest and, the more I read about it, the more I knew it was what I wanted to do. It's my purpose in life." I shove the nacho in my mouth whole and chew, closing my eyes as the lobster, cheese, and salty chip flavors melt in my mouth. *Fantastic.*

I open my eyes to find him staring at me. "Sorry, did you want the last nacho?"

He laughs. "Little late to ask."

"We could get another order."

"I'm fine. It's cool what you're doing with your life."

I nod. "I'm pretty excited about CRISPR research in particular. Have you heard of it? It's editing actual genes. They're working on using a patient's own immune system to fight cancer."

"Haven't heard of it. Tell me more."

So I do. I can talk biomedical stuff for hours. And he actually seems interested and is following along, asking thoughtful questions. I've never had anyone in my life listen to me about my passion so well, except for Sara.

We talk for hours, until the bar closes. I'm not so tipsy anymore after sitting here for so long. Brendan told me about his family's construction and real estate development business back in Brooklyn. I grew up in Brooklyn, so we talked about that for a bit too, arguing good-naturedly over the best places to go for pizza, bagels, and almost any country's food you could possibly want. Brooklyn's neighborhoods are a melting pot of nationalities. He grew up in a much nicer neighborhood than I did. Sara did the best she could for me with her two jobs and a piddly monthly check from our uncle after he abandoned us for Nashville dreams. He never did make it big. Serves him right. Not that I'm bitter.

"I'll call for a car," he says, pulling out his phone.

They're probably still playing poker upstairs, but the bar closes to give the bartender a break when it's slow like this.

He tucks his phone in his pocket. "You want to wait outside or in here?"

"Let's go outside."

We grab our coats and make our way to the exit. Brendan is quiet now and seems kind of serious. I'm suddenly swamped with concern that I talked too much.

"Is everything okay?" I ask.

"Yeah."

"Did I talk too much about my research?"

He shakes his head, giving me a small smile. "Not at all."

I bite my lower lip. I definitely talked too much. I think I bored him silly. *Way to show him a good time, Chloe. Talking his ear off about your own interests.* I should've asked him more about himself.

He opens one of the glass front doors for me and I step out into the crisp night air. The stars are brilliant in a dark sky, the moon glowing almost full. I wait for him to join me. I'm about to ask what he likes best about his work when he surprises me.

"I'm so impressed by you, Chloe. You're going to make your mark and help so many people. It's...you're extraordinary."

My cheeks flush at the compliment and I look down, embarrassed. "I'm nothing special. There's lots of people doing this kind of work."

He tips my chin up. "You're heroic in your noble cause."

My breath stalls, my heart racing. "Thank you."

He drops his hold and turns away. I'm surprised at how disappointed I am.

"What do you like about your work?" I ask.

He shakes his head. "It's not the same as yours, I'll tell you that. I was born into the family business. I never even considered doing something different."

"Do you not like it?"

"No, I do. I like working with my brothers and the crew. I can't complain."

"What do you like best about it?"

"I like working with tools. More recently, I scout out properties for development."

"That's cool too. People always need someplace to live and work."

He blows out a breath. "Yeah, I guess."

Shit. I thought we were having a fun night, but now he seems down because he thinks my work is important and maybe his isn't.

"Everyone does what they're good at," I say. "I'd be shit trying to use a drill or whatever it is you do with pipes, and I'd be too scared to touch a wire."

He chuckles. "You're sweet, but there's lots of people who could do my job."

"Mine too."

He shakes his head in disbelief.

"It's true! No one works in a vacuum. There's a global scientific community out there just like there's a global construction workforce. The world needs all kinds of people in all kinds of jobs."

He grins. "Just when I was thinking you weren't a fiery redhead, you show me some spirit."

I stare at him, trying for a comeback and coming up short. I'm blond and there's nothing wrong with that. He's so hung up on redheads. Maybe an ex?

Our car pulls up, a silver Mercedes, and the driver gets out, opening the back door for us. "Thank you, Eli," I say. I've been here enough to know the drivers.

"You're welcome," he says warmly.

Once we're settled in the backseat, Brendan seems to perk up. "I guess you'll be studying some more tonight, eh?" He's teasing me again. I want to prove him wrong. I can have fun for an extended period. Or at least two days of my three-week winter break.

"Nope. Not tonight."

"No?" he asks with a smile in his voice. "But, Chloe, it's past midnight. Don't you turn into a pumpkin?"

"Are you trying to piss me off?"

"It's kinda fun to hear you live up to your hair."

I grab the ends of my shoulder-length hair and toss it in the air. "What is it with you and redheads?"

He claws at the air. "They're passionate."

"I can be passionate. Sex is just biology and completely natural. I have zero hangups or inhibitions about it." *Fact.*

"Are you still drunk?" His voice sounds strangled.

"No, it seems to have worn off. I had fun tonight. Will you be around tomorrow?"

He stares straight ahead. "I leave early tomorrow morning."

Oh. I guess this is goodbye.

Dammit. I don't want the fun to end.

I study his profile. His jaw is tense, but then I get distracted by his sensual lips. I'm itching to touch his short beard. Soft or coarse? What would it feel like rubbing against me? I've never kissed a man with a beard.

Brendan's earlier words come back to me: *that would be like kissing my cousin. So wrong.*

I turn away, looking out the window. I need to stop lusting for him. Tonight he acted more like an overprotective big brother than a guy who's lusting for me.

We drive the rest of the way in silence, but it's a thick silence, almost like a question hanging in the air—will the fun continue? Or maybe that's just me. I'm not ready for our time together to end.

Once we're inside the palace, we head for the stairs leading to our rooms, still quiet. I catch him looking at me a few times, probably because I'm sneaking peeks at him.

We reach his room first. He stops in front of his door. "I'd offer to walk you to your room, but you said you could make it there on your own. Before, I mean."

I search his features, his thick lashes framing the bluest of blue eyes. There's a scar by his right eyebrow, a thin line. The only visible imperfection. I suddenly want to rip his clothes off and check him over for more. *Oh my God. Cool it.*

Then again, he's leaving tomorrow morning, and I'll never have to see him again.

No. We said we were doing the friend thing. It's just that he's so hot and he's making *me* hot.

"Goodnight, Chloe. See ya around Villroy."

I rub the side of my neck. "Yeah. See ya." I take a step back, even though everything in me wants to get closer.

Screw this.

I close the distance, grab his head, and kiss him.

He's not kissing me back. At all.

I let him go, my face flaming. "Sorry."

"Yeah," he mutters, grabbing the doorknob behind him and opening the door. "'Night."

And then he's gone.

I cover my face with my hands, so mortified I can't even move. *What's wrong with me?*

I drop my hands and stare off in the distance. Geez, he was a good friend to me when I needed one. Didn't I learn my lesson with Michael? Friends with benefits ruins friendships.

I hurry down the hall to my room. I can only hope I don't have to see him again until next Christmas. I'll stay glued to Sara's side the entire visit. I can't bear to face him again one-on-one. Hopefully, a year will be enough time for him to forget all about that unwanted kiss.

6

Six months later…

Brendan

I don't like living alone as much as I thought I would. My whole life I've lived with one brother or another. My current roommate, Beast, is house-sitting for our older brother Sean and his actress wife, Josie, while they're off in Vancouver for a movie she's in. Some kind of mystery, where she plays one of the suspects. That's all she can share. Anyway, I can't blame Beast for taking them up on their offer to house-sit. They live in a ritzy brownstone in the Park Slope neighborhood of Brooklyn. They even have a theater room with a huge screen that drops down from the ceiling by remote control. So it's just me on a Saturday afternoon, watching TV and trying not to dwell on the fact that I'm solo.

My mind drifts to Chloe, as it often does in a moment of quiet. Okay, I'm man enough to admit it, I haven't had as much fun with a woman since Christmas in Villroy with her. There. I said it. (In my head. No one needs to know that embarrassing shit.) I don't know why she lingers in my mind, considering how different we are. I mean, yeah, she's damn nice to look at and I admire her brains too. The great thing about a smart woman is you can count on her to have a rational, thoughtful take on things, instead of a big uncomfortable emotional outburst. She'd never throw a pointy stiletto at my head while she bawls her eyes out over me like *some* women. *Mallory.*

At the same time, I turned Chloe down for a good reason. Walking away from her that night was the hardest thing I've ever done.

Still, I find myself wondering how she's doing. I looked up how to get into Harvard Medical School. Did she do well on the MCAT? (That's the med school admissions test.) Is she happy? Is she single?

Not my business.

I get off the sofa, restless. It's a sunny June day. I should go for a run, burn up some calories in anticipation of drinking at a bar tonight. I'll see who's around to go out later. I grab my sneakers from the bedroom, sit on the end of the bed, and lace up. Strange how unappealing the bar pickup scene's been recently.

I open the front door and jog downstairs just as someone's coming up with a pile of boxes stacked higher than their head. It's definitely a woman judging by the small hands.

"Lemme help you with that," I say.

She halts and peeks around the boxes. "I got it."

I freeze. Her hair is blond, but I know that face. Those green eyes, her fine features, the bow in her top lip. "Chloe?"

"Brendan?"

"What're you doing here?" we say at the same time.

I laugh. "I live here."

"Me too. Just for the summer."

I take the top two boxes off the pile, leaving her with one, and head back upstairs. "Second or third floor?"

"Second."

Adrenaline fires through me. That's where I live. There's four apartments on the second floor, and my next-door neighbors, a couple, just left yesterday to spend the summer at his family's home in Italy. Chloe is moving in right next door to me.

Holy hell.

Questions race through my mind—how did she end up my neighbor? What's she doing this summer? Does she remember that kiss?

"Did you know I lived here?" I ask.

Her brows shoot up. "No. Sara arranged for the apartment for me. The couple went to Italy for the summer."

"Yeah, that's the Malones."

How am I supposed to resist temptation when she's right there?

I remind myself why I resisted her in the first place. Our family connection. It's probably how she ended up here. My cousin Phillip is the one who let us know about this building. The owner is a friend of his. Phillip knows just about everyone as the UN Ambassador for Clean Water. I bet Sara found out about the open apartment through her husband, who asked his brother.

This is bad. I can't be the reason there's another fallout between the Villroy and Brooklyn Rourkes. It would kill my dad not to be welcome in his kingdom. When you're raised to be king, the kingdom is everything.

I stop in front of her door and wait for her to unlock it. "I live right next door."

She keeps her focus on the door, but I don't miss the way her entire body tenses. "Small world."

"It's the family connection. Phillip told us about this building. That's probably where Sara heard about it." I follow her in and set the boxes down inside. She sets her box next to them, takes her laptop off her shoulder, and lays it on top of the light wood coffee table.

I rub my hands together. "Anything else?"

"Just my suitcase."

"I got it." I head down and grab a large black wheeled suitcase from where she left it in the foyer. I can't believe she's living right next door to me. Do I ignore her? But what if she wants to hang out as friends like we did in Villroy? I can't be rude if she asks, especially after I rejected her kiss. I so wanted to follow through. This is what happens when you do the right thing. It bites you in the ass later. *You thought that was a test of willpower? How's this?*

I push open her unlocked door and set her suitcase inside. This is a one-bedroom apartment, and I happen to know her bedroom shares a wall with mine. Let's just say I've heard the mattress next door creaking with newlywed action. I had to get earplugs.

Chloe looks around the place, seeming pleased. It's cozy with a beige upholstered sofa, a couple of curved wooden chairs, and assorted wood tables. There's a series of large framed black-and-white pictures from the Malones' wedding in Italy on the wall. Classy.

"So, what's new?" I ask.

She spreads her arms wide. "Not much. Starting my internship at a lab on Monday."

"How long is your internship?"

"Eight weeks. Then I'll visit Sara on Villroy until it's time to go back to college."

Eight weeks. That's long enough to really get tangled up in someone. If you were looking for a relationship, that is. Which I'm not. The real problem here is that eight weeks is long enough to be way too tempted to cross the line. Which I'm also not.

Is she still in touch with her psycho ex? The one who threatened death if I touched her?

Who cares? It's not like he'd fly all the way to Brooklyn to kill me. Pretty sure.

An awkward silence stretches between us while I try to figure out the right thing to say to the woman I've worked hard to forget.

"How'd school go last semester?" I blurt.

She twirls a lock of soft-looking shoulder-length blond hair and looks toward the door. "Fine."

Does she want me to leave?

"Did you do well on the MCAT?"

She tilts her head. "You know about the MCAT?"

"Yeah, a friend of mine took it," I mutter, lying through my teeth. I don't know anyone who went to medical school besides my doctor. But I never asked her about the process. Whatever.

"I'm happy with my score," she says, gripping her hands together in front of her.

I stare at her gripped hands, and she shifts, gripping them behind her back instead. She's wearing an emerald green tank top, jeans, and white Keds. Just like I remember her wearing back on Villroy. She's big on the tank top-jeans combo, though she added a cardigan there. My gaze catches on the dip between her collarbones, the line of her neck, her delicate-looking jaw.

I suddenly realize I'm staring too long and not holding up my end of the conversation. "Good. That's good. Are you hungry? We could…" I gesture toward the door.

"Not really. I had lunch a couple of hours ago."

I nod. *Makes sense. It is afternoon.* "Need any help unpacking?" *Just your neighborly helper here.*

She crosses her arms and uncrosses them. "It's just my research papers and notebooks. I can do it myself."

I rub the back of my neck. *Why is this so hard?* She's just a woman I had some friendly good times with. A friend. My only woman friend ever. "So, I'm right next door. Knock if ya need anything."

"Okay." She walks to the door.

Guess that's my cue to leave.

"See ya." I let myself out.

Then I just stand in the hallway for a moment, my head spinning. Could that have been more awkward? I need to figure out how to be neighbors with her. I don't want to spend the summer tuned into every sound next door, thinking about what she's doing, or who she's doing it with.

Shit. Am I going to have to hear her hooking up with a guy?

I jog downstairs, more agitated with every step. This is *not* going to work. I have to figure something out fast.

I wonder if I could move in with Beast. No. That's the coward's way. This is my place. And Chloe Travers isn't going to force me out. No matter how awkward things get.

～

Chloe

I walk to the small galley kitchen in a daze. Brendan Rourke. The guy I hoped not to see face-to-face for a very long time is right next door. I reach for a glass with a shaky hand and pour myself some water from the sink. That was so freaking awkward. He must've remembered that unwanted kiss. I'm just so…mortified. He's probably thinking, *Shit, the woman who lusts for me is right next door. Now I'll have to dodge her advances all summer.*

If he only knew. After careful consideration of the facts, I've concluded the reason he's my go-to fantasy with my vibrator, Blaze, is because my mind conjured a different ending to that night in Villroy. Purely in self-defense. In my fantasy version, he returns my kiss and pulls me into his room. Many orgasms follow. *Thank you, Blaze.*

I exhale sharply. No one ever needs to know that, especially my new neighbor. The fact that he pops into my mind with his sparkling blue eyes, ready smile, and appealing dimple on a regular basis is also easy to understand. He was a bright spot during a vulnerable, lonely time over the holidays. Another theory I have is that when I'm overworked like I was this past semester, my mind goes back to the last time I had fun. He was so fun. Two plausible theories to explain why I can't seem to forget him. It makes sense when you look at it objectively. Well, there's no forgetting him now! He's right *there*.

Did Sara know he lived in this building?

I send her a quick text letting her know I got in okay. Then I ask her about Brendan.

Sara: *Brendan who?*

She didn't know. It's the family connection through Phillip just like Brendan said.

Me: *Brendan Rourke lives next door.*

Sara: …

She's probably checking in with Adrian about it. It's night in Villroy, which means they're both at work at the casino they co-own and run.

I bring my water to the sofa and sink down heavily.

Sara: *Adrian says it's most likely the Phillip connection. Phillip's friend owns the building. It's cool though, right? You hung out with Brendan in Villroy last Christmas. Instant friend.*

I never told her about my unwanted advance. Too embarrassing.

Me: *Yeah, we hung out before.*

Sara: *Great! Now at least I know you won't be all work, no play this summer. Have fun! Tell him Adrian and I say hi. Gotta go. Love you!*

I text a quick "love you too" back and set my phone on the coffee table. I glance toward the shared wall with Brendan's place, adrenaline firing through me. Distraction time.

A few minutes later, I'm knee-deep in papers and notebooks as I unpack my boxes. I was lucky to land an eight-week internship focused on cancer genome dynamics at a cancer center affiliated with NYU in the city. This summer is all about work. I'm going to do my research, spend some time putting together med school applications, and study to get a jump on next semester. With my heavy course load, it helps to get a running start. My vibrator will get a lot of action but hey. At least Blaze doesn't distract me once we're done. He's earned the name Blaze for the smoking hot race to the finish. In fact, I'll use him tonight to take the edge off.

Feeling a little better, I organize a study space for myself using a long side table covered in picture frames. I relocate the frames to some of the end tables scattered around the living room. I hang my work clothes in the bedroom closet—a few skirts and blouses I can mix and match—and put the rest of my clothes in the two drawers left empty for me.

After I finish organizing my stuff, I go out for groceries and head back to my new place. This isn't too far from where I grew up, so I'm pretty comfortable finding my way around. I put the food away, sit on the sofa, and try to decide what to do first. Should I make dinner? Review the published work of the research director I'll be working under? Or do I address the problem living next door?

I need to clear the air with Brendan. I'll feel him out, see if he remembers that kiss, and, if he does, I'll assure him there's no worries from this end. Maybe I'll claim I was drunk that night. No, I'm pretty sure I told him the buzz had worn off by the end of the night. Why am I so direct and honest all the time? It's a curse. I'm definitely not hanging with him this summer and risking acting on my unwanted lusty impulses. He's way too appealing to torture myself like that. I just need to stop worrying about the elephant in the room. Right? *Ready, set, go next door!*

I wander to the kitchen, procrastinating the next-door neighbor problem. It's near dinnertime. I'll make a box of mac 'n cheese with a salad. I find a pot, fill it with water, and set it on the stovetop. I sigh. *Not feeling it.* I'm hungry, but not in the mood to cook. I could get takeout. There's a stipend with my internship and I don't have any other expenses this summer. Sara covered my rent, saying it was part of my education. She's taken care of me my whole life, but now that she has a family of her own, I'm determined to pay for med school, even if it means taking out student loans. She has Henry now and needs to invest in his education.

I pace the apartment, working up my nerve to face the guy next door. He's just a guy. This doesn't have to be a big deal.

I'll go for a walk.

Halfway to the door, I hear a sound in the hallway and still, my heart picking up speed. Is it Brendan? I can't go out now. It'll look like I'm trying to run into him.

I slide both hands through my hair and close my eyes. This is nuts. *Don't be a wuss.*

A knock on my door startles me. Is it him? It's got to be someone who lives in the building. Otherwise, they'd have to be buzzed in through the intercom. Maybe he had the same idea that we should clear the air. The awkward factor was off the charts. He had to have noticed it.

I go over and peek through the peephole.

It's him.

I pull the door open. "Hi." That's all I've got.

Brendan leans against the doorframe and crosses his arms, his snug blue T-shirt hugging his biceps. His forearms are corded and muscular. And he's in faded jeans. I love the look of jeans on a guy's ass. Yup, my lust for him stays strong. This is so embarrassing.

I meet his sky blue eyes gleaming devilishly, a hint of a smile playing about his mouth, revealing his dimple, barely visible through his short beard. Just like I remember.

"Hey," he says.

"Hey."

This is going well.

I take a deep breath. "So," I say at the same time as he says, "I thought…"

"You go ahead," we say at the same time.

I laugh a little. "This is weird, isn't it? I swear I didn't know you lived here." I hold my palms up. "It doesn't have to be awkward. I'm perfectly capable of keeping to myself. You won't even know I'm here."

He straightens. "You don't have to hide out or anything."

I worry my lower lip, unsure if I should bring up the unwanted kiss and assure him I'll never do that again. Maybe he forgot?

An awkward silence settles between us.

He looks over my shoulder and does a double take. "What is that?"

I glance back. "It's my study space."

He stares. "What is that ugly thing with the wrinkled face and blue hair sticking straight up?"

I laugh. "That's my troll doll. They bring good luck. He goes with me everywhere."

A smile tugs at his lips. "Troll doll, huh? What's its name?"

"Kablooey."

He flashes a smile that lights up his face. "Because his hair looks like it went kablooey." He widens his eyes and explodes his fingers around his hair.

My cheeks flush. "Yeah, and I thought it was a cute way of incorporating blue into a name."

He stares at me for a moment. "You and Kablooey all set for a summer of study, party girl?"

I tense. He called me party girl several times that night at the bar in Villroy, which means he remembers the incident I'm desperate to forget. Attempted seduction fail. I have to deal with this in a mature and responsible way. Then we can put it behind us.

I gesture vaguely behind me. "Yeah, that's my usual mode plus work at the lab, of course. That last night in Villroy got crazy. I never drink. I wasn't myself at all."

His gaze drops to my collarbone. "I remember."

"Yeah. Ha-ha. Wild night! Anyway, back to study mode."

He lifts his gaze, his bluest of blue eyes making my breath catch. I so wish I weren't attracted to him. I hope he can't tell.

"I'll leave you to it," he says, lifting a hand in farewell.

I belatedly remember he started to say something before I blurted all my *no worries about the lusty woman next door* stuff. "What were you going to say before? I cut you off. When you first got here, you said, 'I thought,' and then I interrupted."

His jaw works for a moment before he says, "Nothing."

"But you came over here for a reason, right?"

His lips press together as he shakes his head in denial. "See ya," he mutters, turning and letting himself out.

I cross my arms. That was weird. And I don't think it was just me that made it weird. What's going on in his head?

7

———

Brendan

I head back to my apartment, turn on the TV, and crash on the sofa. That was weird. I thought I'd clear the air so it wouldn't be awkward every time we ran into each other. I planned to say I'd be super busy this summer, but let me know if she needs anything. Neighborly, not too friendly. I needed to set expectations so she didn't think we were going to hang out like we did in Villroy. I'll never get her out of my head if I spend the next eight weeks with her. It'll practically be like living with her.

Anyway, it looks like she's the one who'll be super busy between work and studying with Kablooey. My lips curl up. I hadn't expected her to have a doll of any kind, let alone an ugly-as-sin troll. She probably thinks it's cute. What else is she into?

I turn off the TV in disgust over wasting my time thinking about the woman I swore I'd stop thinking about, and march out the door. I text Beast to see if he's home. Maybe we'll grab a bite for dinner. I'm secretly hoping he'll cook. My little brother is practically a chef with all his skill, and I miss all the great dinners he prepared when he lived with me. Okay, he's not little and he's only two years younger, but I gotta bust his balls. It's what we do. Dude can cook the most amazing stuff.

I'm talking chili, enchiladas, homemade tortellini in cream sauce, paella, steak with mashed potatoes. I don't know where he learned to cook like that. He says he just got some recipes online and started to get a feel for it. I bet he took cooking classes. You should see him with a knife—chop, chop, chop—like a master chef.

I step outside and get his text. *Come on over.*

Half an hour later, I climb the steps to a corner brownstone in Park Slope and ring the bell. It's my brother Sean's place with his wife, Josie. Beast is house-sitting. He answers the door wearing a red apron over a gray T-shirt and jeans. "Great timing. I'm making enchiladas."

My mouth waters. "Awesome." I follow him downstairs to the kitchen, where there's a large center island with swivel stools that have intricate ironwork decorating the back. This place is so cool. I know Sean did most of the renovation work on it, but it's Josie who decorated it. She's got big bucks now with a couple of movies under her belt. No wonder Beast wanted to house-sit. The kitchen has top-of-the-line appliances, unlike the kitchen at our place.

He opens the refrigerator and pulls out a beer for me, opening it, and handing it over.

"Thanks."

"Yup." He takes a sip of his beer and turns back to the stove, stirring something.

I stare at his bulky shoulders. "You still lifting weights?" He had to leave his dumbbells at our place.

He glances over his shoulder at me. "Yeah, Sean's got weights in the basement."

I cup my hands over my mouth. "Bee-ee-ast."

"Yeah, yeah. Sue me for liking being fit."

I consider telling him about my new neighbor. He knows her from Villroy, but then what would I say? The pretty redhead is living next door and we're friends, but not really. He'll want to know why I don't make a move since I talked about her before like I was into her. How can I explain a casual hookup won't work with our family connection, and I can't risk screwing up a relationship? I'm not even sure I know how to have a relationship. I never have before. And who could forget her psycho assassin ex? I'm sure I'll be seeing him at my next visit to Villroy. Maybe even with Chloe around too. It all comes back to the family connection.

I won't bring it up.

I take a pull on my beer. "Whatcha doing tonight?"

"Hitting up a bar later with the guys for some pool." He turns off the burner and takes out a long baking dish from a cabinet in the island. "Next weekend me and the guys are going to a music festival in Delaware." He's really into travelling around to music festivals. He always meets a ton of women too.

"Cool." I could join him for pool. I know his friends, but I'm not in the mood for the bar scene. I'm friends with a couple of guys on crew, and we usually hit up underground parties in the city—some of them get pretty wild—but that doesn't appeal either.

Well, I'm not going to sit home with *her* next door studying her big brain out. I bet she's home every night studying, which means I'll *have* to go out every night. I'm exhausted just thinking about it. Sometimes a guy just wants to sit home with a beer and watch the game.

"Guess who moved in next door?" I say louder than I mean to.

He stops layering the enchiladas to stare at me. "Mallory?" My ex who bawled her eyes out after our three-week *whatever it was* ended. I thought it was just casual hookups. She thought it was a relationship. Nightmare.

"No," I say. "Geez, that would be bad. That's stalker territory."

"You sound agitated. That's the only woman you ever mentioned who seemed to make an impression."

"Yeah, because she threw a stiletto at my head."

He chuckles and turns, layering the enchilada dish with stuff he has lined up on the counter.

"Besides, how do you know it's a woman living next door?"

He doesn't bother turning around. "If it was a guy, you

would've told me already. Instead you're beating around the bush." He looks over his shoulder at me with a knowing smirk.

He's smart about people. So irritating. "Okay, fine. It's Adrian's sister-in-law."

He doesn't respond, focused on his work.

"The redhead from Villroy."

"Uh-huh."

I wave a hand through the air. "Just moved right on in next door. Now I have to deal with her studying there all the damn time." I tip my bottle back, swallow down a fine IPA, and slam the bottle on the counter. "It's Phillip's friend's building, so there's that family connection making us neighbors. No warning from Phillip either. I should call him."

"Uh-huh."

"I mean, it's just not right. We're cousins. How hard is it to text: *guess what, Chloe Travers is moving in next door for the summer*. Seriously!"

Silence.

I watch as he finishes up the dish and slides it into the oven. He sets the timer, turns, and crosses his arms, pinning me with another knowing look.

"What?" I ask, already feeling defensive.

"Does Phillip believe Chloe is a shady character? Potential criminal element?"

I twist my mouth to the side. "No." He's teasing, but I get it. Why would Phillip think it was a problem to do a favor for another member of the family? He probably knows Chloe better than he knows me or my brothers. "Still, a heads-up would've been nice."

"What's the problem? You're agitated because your neighbor studies a lot?"

I slice a hand through the air. "A guy should have some warning. That's all I'm saying."

He cocks his head. "She shot you down, huh?"

"No. We're friends."

He grins. "Right. Because you have so many women friends."

"Fuck you. I could have a woman friend if I wanted to."

He hides a smile behind his beer and takes a sip. "Glad to hear you're evolving."

I jab a finger at him. "Ya know, if you weren't cooking enchiladas, I'd be outta here."

He walks to the stool adjacent to mine, pulls it out, and takes a seat. "Tell me about the redhead."

"She's blond now."

"Strike one."

"No, it's…fine." *Angelic.* I frown as another problem comes to mind. "Her bedroom shares a wall with mine."

"And?"

"So I'm gonna hafta hear her with random guys!"

"And that's a problem because…"

I glare at him.

"Hmm…friends don't let friends hook up with other guys?"

I sock his shoulder. "Shut up."

"Okay, you have permission to take my bedroom until I'm back, which Sean and Josie say will be around mid-July. Problem solved."

"It's not just that."

"Then what, Romeo?"

I open my mouth and shut it again, at a loss for words. I don't know if I'm coming or going where she's concerned. I just know that I'm spending way too much time thinking about her.

"Bren."

I turn to him. "What?"

"Just ask her out already."

"It's complicated." I take a long swallow of cold beer. I need to keep Chloe at a distance. There's too much potential fallout. But how can I when she's so close?

He stares at me for a moment, and I work on my poker face. Finally, he says, "You hooked up with her, didn't you? Back in Villroy." He leans back in his seat, crossing his arms over his massive chest. "I see what's going on here. You've got a girl you thought you said goodbye to forever living next door, so now it's awkward. You don't want her to get too close because she'll get the wrong idea and think there's something more."

"Nothing happened in Villroy. I told ya we're just friends."

He takes a pull on his beer. "Then you won't mind if I stop by and ask her out, would ya?"

"No!"

He grins and leans forward. "Gotcha."

I scowl. "Not funny."

He chuckles. "Kinda is."

And he doesn't say another word about it. He doesn't have to. He knows and I know that I'm hung up on Chloe. She's the first woman I ever *really* listened to and enjoyed talking with. I have this strange urge to make her happy just to see her smile. It's a stronger urge than even my lusty impulses, which is not how I usually operate. The fact is, I care enough about her I'm not going to get in her way. She needs to focus on her studies. She's going to do great things with her life. I'd just be a distraction.

And isn't that the most important reason to keep my distance? Beyond the family connection fallout, her ex, and the almost certain fact that I'd screw up a relationship—I'm never going to do anything as great as she is with her life. She's made it clear that she has a long, hard journey ahead of her with no space for a relationship. It's why she turned down her ex's proposal. Chloe is on a quest. And my job is to step aside, keeping the path clear for her to continue on her heroic journey.

The only logical solution to her neighborly temptation is for me to go out as much as possible. Just never be home. I'm tired just thinking about it, but it's the right thing to do.

~

Chloe

It's Friday night, and I'm trying to relax after an exhausting first week at my internship. Of course I'm grateful just to be part of any research at such a cutting-edge facility. On the other hand, the lead researcher, Dr. Ruhan, doesn't know me well and started me on the most mind-numbingly rote work. I know you have to start at the bottom, every person on the team has an important role, *blah, blah, blah*. But I was doing more advanced work in high school. On Monday, I hope to get a moment to remind her of my research credentials. I've already been published as co-author with professors in two medical journals.

I set my empty bowl of ramen on the coffee table and flip channels restlessly. Giving up, I turn off the TV. I hear footsteps going down the hallway and my ears perk up. Is it Brendan? He doesn't seem to be home much. I'm here every night after work, and I never hear anything from next door. I think he goes out every night. Not like it's my business.

I'll read. There's plenty of research coming out of the cancer center where I'm working that I haven't read yet. I get my laptop, a glass of water, and curl up on the sofa for a deep dive into science. Three articles later, I'm actually tenser than I was when I got home. Maybe some music would help? Or I could get Blaze to take the edge off with a nice solid orgasm. Now there's a plan.

I head to the bedroom, lock the door, even though it's just me here, strip out of my jeans and panties, and climb in bed. I'm feeling more relaxed already. I pull Blaze out of the nightstand and let him work his magic. *Ahhh, yeah, that is good.* I close my eyes, pleasure spiraling through me. Sky blue eyes gleam in my mind and my eyes fly open in alarm. Brendan can't be part of the fantasy anymore. He's right next door! I'm trying to forget he exists! Who else do I got? I search my mental inventory and settle on that swaggering guy from *The Fast and the Furious*.

Ahhh...so much better. I close my eyes again, settling into the mattress. A sexy smile with a dimple flashes through my mind. *Next!* Manly form leaning against my doorframe, arms crossed, bulging biceps. Okay, okay. Let's face facts. I haven't been with a guy in a while. That's the only reason my mind keeps going back to Brendan, the last guy I spent time with. I don't need a guy. That's why I have Blaze.

I'll just keep my eyes open and focus on Blaze. A wonderful invention for the independent woman. Back to business. Serious stuff. I stare at the ceiling, refusing to think of *him*, waiting for the pleasure to return. At this rate, I'm going to run out of battery power. *Oh. Okay. Getting there.*

Yes. Yes. Yes. Faster, faster. I need to outrun memories. More power, Blaze!

I cry out harshly as my release slams into me. I pant as I ease back to reality, slowing down the vibrating power and finally turning it off.

A sharp knock on the front door startles me. I uncouple from my trusty boyfriend, leap out of bed, and quickly dress. My panties are damp, but what can you do. Hopefully I don't look like I just got off.

Another knock.

It has to be a neighbor. *Is it him?*

What am I doing? I can't answer the door post-orgasm if it's him. I'll say I had headphones on and didn't hear the knock. Curiosity gets the better of me. I tiptoe over and peek through the peephole.

Brendan.

I scramble back, my bare ankle slamming into the hard edge of the wood coffee table leg. I yelp in pain and nearly lose my balance but manage to right myself.

"Chloe, are you okay?" he calls through the door. He sounds concerned.

I cringe. *Now I have to answer the door.*

"Yes," I call out. "Just a minute."

I smooth my hair, take a deep breath, and open the door. "Hey, what's up?"

Brendan immediately looks over my shoulder. "What happened?"

"Nothing. I nicked my ankle on the coffee table." I lift my ankle behind me, glance back, and quickly drop it. There's a thin line of blood from the scrape. Somehow those surface cuts hurt like hell. All those nerve endings protesting, I guess.

He peers around my shoulder. "Mind if I come in?"

"Sure."

He steps inside, his dark brown hair damp from the shower. He smells like soap and that woodsy scent that nearly makes my eyes roll back in my head. Snug white T-shirt, faded jeans, sneakers. *Is he trying to tempt me? Because I'm into the multi-orgasm night. Wrong. So wrong.*

He walks over to the kitchen and peers down the short hallway toward my bedroom. *Shit.* Did he hear me in there? Is he looking for the guy? Just a solo endeavor! That's not any better, is it?

Play it cool. Maybe he doesn't know. Maybe he's just curious how my apartment is laid out compared to his.

"Need something?" I ask casually.

He stills and then glances around my kitchen, gesturing toward my refrigerator. "Just wondering if you had the same ancient refrigerator as I do. I planned to mention an upgrade to the landlord." He plants his hands on his hips and stares at my refrigerator.

I shift uneasily. "So, okay. An upgrade would be nice."

He slowly turns to me. "Yeah." He rubs the back of his neck. "So…" He ambles out of the kitchen, his brows drawn together.

I watch, expecting him to amble out the door, but he stops suddenly and turns to me. A smile tugs at his lips. "Were you, uh, working out? Your cheeks and neck are bright pink."

"Yes! I like to work out after work. Ha. Two works. I'm a *hard* worker. That's how I bumped my ankle." I congratulate myself on this completely reasonable explanation. I'm *so* playing it cool.

"You sure you're okay?" He closes the distance and puts the back of his hand on my forehead, his brows shooting up over twinkling blue eyes. "Chloe, you're burning up."

There's no hope for it. It's post-orgasm heat, raw lust, and embarrassment, a killer combo. Still, I double down on denial. "Just exertion. I was dancing."

He cocks his head. "There's no music, and that night at the bar in Villroy you said you didn't dance."

Great! Bring up that night. Could we pile on any more embarrassment to this moment?

I wave a hand airily, trying to come up with something believable. "It was interpretive dance. You don't need music. It's not officially recognized as a legitimate dance form by the established dance, uh, culture. So, according to those more expert than I, I was technically *not* dancing."

He crosses his arms, his blue eyes dancing with amusement. "Uh-huh. What were you really doing?"

I attempt an interpretive dance move—pumping my fists forward and then straight up a few times. "It's a weekend victory dance. My roommate and I used to do this to celebrate every Friday night."

His lips curve into a sexy smile. "I've got to meet this roommate."

"She's back in Texas for the summer. Just me. So what's new?" I'm nearly bouncing on the balls of my feet. I'm pumped from my recent exertion and the fact that he's here, smiling his sexy smile at me. Not that I'm going to pounce on him or anything. Been there, got the awkward memory to live down forever.

He steps closer, and my pulse kicks up. "What're ya doing tomorrow night, party girl?"

"I don't know. What're we doing?"

He flashes a smile that makes my breath catch. "We're going to *attempt* to cook homemade tortellini. Beast made it before. It's the best I've ever had, and since neither of us is great at cooking, I thought it could be something we figured out together."

We talked about our lack of cooking skill back in Villroy. We talked about a lot of things that night at the bar. Why did I have to ruin it by kissing him? This is my second chance for a real friendship, and I can't blow it. I don't have a lot of close friends, just Sara and my roommate, Lindsey.

I smile. "Sure. Text me to let me know what time." I give him my number, and he texts me back so I'll have his.

He glances at my kitchen. "Your kitchen isn't as big as mine. We'll use mine. I'll pick up the ingredients. It takes a while to make the dough, roll it out, all that. You okay with a few hours' time commitment? I know you've got a lot to cram into that genius head of yours—"

"I can do it."

He smiles warmly, setting off a flutter low in my belly. "Cool."

We stand there staring at each other for a long moment. There's something hypnotizing about his eyes as they change from warm to heated to smoldering. *Wait, what?* My mouth goes dry. Is this not one-sided?

He blinks, gesturing toward the door and easing back a step. "See ya tomorrow."

"We could watch a movie or something if you want to hang out."

"I'm going out, but thanks."

I rub the side of my neck. "Oh. Sure. Have fun." I don't expect an invitation to join him. He's probably cruising for women at a bar. Not my business.

He walks to the door and stops with his hand on the knob. "Did you know our bedrooms share a wall?"

"No," I say slowly as the undeniable truth dawns. *Oh God.*

He grins. "Now you know."

8

Brendan

I'm waiting in line at the grocery store with the tortellini ingredients on Saturday, and I find myself smiling about seeing Chloe later this afternoon. Ridiculous. The only reason I'm looking forward to it is so I can stop wondering what she's doing next door. Yesterday I heard her orgasmic cry when I got out of the shower, so, okay, I got jealous. I went next door to see who the hell she was with. Turns out she was alone. At first I felt awkward, relieved but awkward. Hey, I didn't *want* to hear what I heard. She was so bright pink with embarrassment I couldn't help teasing her. Her excuses were hysterical and frigging adorable. Which is how I decided it wouldn't hurt to spend some time together as friends.

I shift forward in line, my mind conjuring her again—soft blond hair, sharp green eyes, petite curvy body, always in a tank top and jeans. Sometimes she throws a cardigan over the tank, sometimes not. I spend way too much time dwelling on the delicate lines of her collarbones. The bow in her top lip, the fuller lower lip.

I text her, letting her know I'm on my way home with the tortellini stuff. Almost sounds like we share a home. *Shit.* I suddenly wish I could take it back. It sounds too domestic.

Chloe: *I accidentally got your mail in my box. Stopped by your place this morning, but you weren't home. I slid it under your door. Early workout?*

Me: *Ha. No. I haven't made it home yet from last night.*

Chloe: *Sounds like a wild night.*

I think up a noncommittal response. This isn't my first female text rodeo. She's curious what I was up to last night; otherwise, she would've just said *cool* or sent one of those girly emojis. Maybe she wonders if I hooked up with someone. Would it bother her if I did? Fact is, I never spend the night after a hookup anymore. It's just not worth giving a woman false hope that I'm looking for something more. I went to a party last night and then crashed on the couch at a friend's place, who's lucky enough to sublet a rent-stabilized apartment in the city. But Chloe doesn't need to know that.

Me: *Not as wild as yours, I'm sure, party girl.*

No reply.

I scowl at my phone, irritated beyond reason that she didn't reply. I need to stop getting so worked up over her. Chloe's path, while noble, could never gel with mine. She could end up way out in California for all I know with med school and whatever comes after. I'm anchored here with my family's construction business. Yet another reason it's not worth getting tangled up.

And then I see three dots on my phone screen. My pulse kicks up in anticipation.

Chloe: *I'm weirdly looking forward to cooking.*

I smile and text back. *Me too.*

I'm not crossing the line. But I might walk right up to it.

~

Chloe

"Have you ever cracked an egg before?" I ask with a laugh. Brendan is worse in the kitchen than I am.

"Hey, no judgment," he says, picking half the shell out of the center of his flour bowl. We're making homemade dough for the tortellini, which means we have to make a bowl out of the flour and put eggs in the center before we mix. Mine's perfect. It's like a chemistry experiment—the right proportions in the right order give predictable results. I'm waiting for him to finish his egg bowl before we go on to the next step. We're following along with a cooking video on his laptop.

His flour bowl collapses on one side as his big fingers attempt to get the shell out. I push the flour back in place quickly and bump him with my hip. "Move over. Let the expert do the work. It takes the precision of a skilled chemist."

He does a quick backstep and appears at my other side. "What're ya talking about? Mine looks perfect." He points to the flour bowl I created, claiming it as his own.

I shake my head, smiling, and carefully pick the big shell out and then pile the slivers of shell remaining inside it. "Do you have two rolling pins?"

"Err…" He twists his lips to the side. "Kinda forgot the rolling pin thing."

"I'll go back to my place and see if your neighbors left one."

I wash my hands, dry them, and head next door, a bounce in my step. My dreary day took a turn into sunny town the moment I joined Brendan. It's so cozy cooking in his kitchen, rock music playing in the background. He's so fun and funny. I try not to think about the fact that he didn't come home last night. He was a little cagey about it, which I'm sure means he spent the night with a woman. I *have* to be fine with that. Clearly, he's content to get his physical needs met elsewhere. I'm just his neighbor friend.

Back at my place, I rummage around in the cabinets and find a wooden rolling pin. Just one. I guess most people don't own two. That's okay.

Once I'm back at Brendan's place, I hold it up over my head. "Ta-dah!"

He grins and cups his hands over his mouth. "Victory!"

I laugh and bring it over. "We could take turns with it."

"I looked up substitutes. We can use a glass bottle too." He holds up an empty vodka bottle. "I'll roll with this; you roll with the rolling pin."

I study him. Did he get drunk in the few minutes I was gone? There's definitely an alcohol smell in the air. "You didn't just finish that vodka, did you?"

He staggers around comically, slurring his words, "What maketh ya thay dat?" He bumps into me, sending me flying back into the counter, his arm cushioning my back at the last moment. My breath catches, heat flooding my body at the sudden closeness of the man I'm desperately trying not to lust for. Up close, his eyes are clear. Not drunk.

"Sorry," he says, easing back from me. "I forgot how light you are."

I smooth my hair, flustered. "I'm glad you're sober because it's harder to work with a drunk person. I've seen plenty of staggering drunks in college."

"I bet." His voice is rough.

I stare at his broad chest in a black T-shirt, which is at my eye level. He's got a million pounds of muscle on me. The man is *fit* from his wide shoulders to his defined abs to his steel ass. I couldn't help checking out his ass in his faded jeans as he moved around the kitchen earlier. I wish I weren't so drawn to him.

I blink and shove him out of my way. He lets me. "So what did you do with the vodka?"

He stares at me blankly for a moment before turning to the refrigerator and producing an insulated water bottle. "Vodka's new home."

I focus on the bottle instead of the tanned muscular arm holding it. "You should label that. What if you take a swig after a workout? Or Garrett comes back and thinks it's water?" He told me his younger brother is his roommate when he's not house-sitting.

"Ha! That would be hilarious. Takes a lot to bring him down."

I shake my head. "You're terrible."

"Terribly hilarious."

I give his shoulder a nudge. "Label it."

He lifts his palms. "With what?"

"I'll take care of it. I got stuff at my place." I head toward the door, relieved to put some space between us.

"If you keep strutting back to your place, we're never gonna get this pasta into shape."

I nearly stumble. I slowly turn back to him. "Sorry, strutting?"

"Yeah, the Chloe walk." He executes a bouncy step, throwing in a few hip swivels as he goes.

I crack up, even though he's making fun. "Stop. I don't look that bad."

He waggles his brows. "You look that good." He swivels his finger in the air. "Go ahead and turn around, commence strutting."

"Don't watch." I turn back toward the door and work on walking as normally as possible, no bounce, no sway.

"Now you look like you have a stick up your ass."

I throw my hands in the air and hear his low laugh. He's big on teasing.

I laugh a little to myself as I gather up the stuff from my apartment—Post-it, pen, tape. When I return to his place, his back's to me and he's dancing, one hand on the back of his neck, the other arm going back and forth as he slowly turns. He's doing the Sprinkler.

I stop and slap a hand over my mouth to hold in the sound of my laughter. I watch, thrilled I've got something to tease him about now. He keeps dancing, slowly turning, until he catches my eye. He immediately drops his arm and runs a hand through his hair in a casual gesture. "Oh, hey. You're back."

"What were you doing?" I ask, fighting a laugh.

"I'll tell you what I *wasn't* doing. I wasn't dancing."

I giggle as I approach. His expression is pure innocence. He's outrageous.

"Oh, no? What do ya call it?"

"Interpretive dance," he says with a straight face. "Not officially recognized by dance culture."

I gape at him. My own words from last night after he

caught me post-vibrator action, all flushed with endorphins. Here I thought I caught him in an embarrassing act, but he was just teasing me from before. My cheeks flame.

He winks.

I palm his face and shove. He grabs my wrist and shifts away, laughing.

In a futile effort to hold the mortification at bay, I keep my focus on my label work, carefully printing "vodka" in all capital letters on the Post-it. Then I tape it to the water bottle. I help myself to a chilled bottled water, too, in hopes of cooling down the seemingly never-ending inferno of embarrassment I keep finding myself in around him.

He lets out an exaggerated sigh, leaning against the counter and crossing his arms over his broad chest. "Can we please get back to work? I'd like to eat before nine o'clock."

"What a taskmaster. Work, work, work." I set my water on the counter and join him back at our flour bowls. "All right, hit play on Massimo. Let's make some dough." That's the chef we're following in the video.

"That sounds like we're gonna get rich."

"Tortellini rich. Let's go, pokey."

Brendan hits play and the dulcet rhythm of Massimo's Italian accent instructing us in English returns. But all I can focus on is the woodsy masculine scent from the man at my side, the heat radiating off him, his corded muscular forearms as his hands rest on the counter, awaiting instruction.

I desperately want those hands on me. Why can't I just relax and enjoy our friendship? I learned my lesson with Michael. Once you cross the line, that friendship is gone. Not that Brendan has shown any interest. He jokes around with me like he does with his brothers. I'm sure with a woman he's interested in, he's all smooth moves and charm. Like with whoever he was with last night. Now if that doesn't cool my lust, nothing will.

It's for the best. I need to stay focused on my work. Friends can pick up again whenever, but a relationship, that's different. I've avoided them because I know it takes work to make time to see each other, to be there for each other, and the long distance with me off at medical school soon would be tough. I have no control over which med school I get into. Harvard is my dream, but I have to cast a wide net with my applications. I'll look for someone to get serious with after my medical training. Now is for fun.

"Paging Dr. Travers," Brendan says.

I startle and realize he paused the video. It must be time for us to do the next step and I missed it. "Yes?"

"We have to whisk the eggs, but I don't have a whisk."

"I know what to do."

"Are you about to strut back to your place for a whisk?"

I elbow him in the ribs, and he makes an exaggerated *oof* sound, wincing and bending over. "Damn, Chloe, have you been lifting weights with pencils again?" He grabs my pen from the counter and does an arm curl like it's a dumbbell, patting the bulge of his bicep with his other hand. I don't know whether to laugh or reach out to feel the hard curve of muscle. He grins at me, his blue eyes sparkling devilishly.

I pull two forks from a drawer and hand him one. "Get whisking."

We stand side by side, whisking the eggs in the center of our flour bowls.

"What's next again?" I ask since I was distracted during the video.

"We have to gradually push the flour into the center to mix it."

"Got it."

"You totally spaced when Massimo told us all this. What were you thinking about?"

Sex. "Neurogenetics."

"Ah. Me too."

I laugh.

He nudges my shoulder with his. "What? You think you cornered the market on neurogenetics daydreaming? Nuh-uh. It's all I can think about."

I shake my head, smiling. "I'm sure."

We finish up whisking and cave in the bowls, making a mess of the dough.

"Are you sure this is going to turn into pasta?" I ask. "It looks awful."

"Give it time. Massimo says he helped make this when he was a kid. I'm sure two adults can handle it." He grins. "We can always call for pizza."

~

Two hours later, we've got the meat filling on top of a bunch of square pieces of pasta, and we're working on making the little tortellini pouches. I'm having a blast.

"Are your feet hurting?" he asks. "Mine are."

"A bit."

He goes to the other side of a half-wall countertop that separates the kitchen from the living room and retrieves two cushioned black stools for us to sit on.

"I should've thought of that," I say, taking a seat. We've been on our feet for hours.

"You were distracted by Massimo and neurogenetics," he says, sitting next to me. "Aren't we all?"

I smile and keep working on my cute pouches of pasta. "I think we made too much. We're going to have hundreds of these little buggers."

"You can never have too much pasta."

"Uh, yeah, you can. Too many carbs and you'll puff out like the Pillsbury Doughboy."

"He should totally stop eating himself. Ooh, that sounds dirty. Naughty Chloe."

I roll my eyes.

He's quiet for a moment as he works. "I heard it's tough to get into Harvard Medical School. Do you have a plan B?"

I still. *He looked into it?* I glance over at him, but his focus is on his pasta, so I return to my own pasta. "Yeah, it's tough. It's my goal, but, of course, I'll apply other places."

"Where?"

I glance over, surprised he wants to know. I've still got a year left at Columbia. Does he expect we'll still be hanging out by the time med school rolls around? That's kinda nice that he cares so much about our friendship. "Johns Hopkins, Penn—"

"NYU?"

"Yeah, I'll apply there. Also, Stanford."

"That's in California. NYU's a great school. So's Columbia." Those last two are in New York. Aww, he wants us to keep hanging out. It's so sweet.

"I know," I say softly. "I'll apply there too. But my first choice is Harvard."

"And after that?"

"I'll do my residency, and then I hope to get a fellowship at a top cancer research center."

"Which could be someplace besides where you go to medical school?"

"Yes. It's a whole other application process."

He shakes his head. "That's a lot of hard work to reach your goal. Probably a lot of moving around too."

I lift my gaze to his in question.

His eyes are serious, though he keeps his tone light. "Not as hard as making tortellini, but still."

There's a definite tension in the air, something that wasn't there before. I don't know what to do about it, so I ignore it. I can't change who I am, and it's better if he knows that up front.

"Speaking of tortellini," I say, breaking the tense silence, "I've got like a thousand here compared to your measly twenty-one."

"Oh, you noticed my pyramid of greatness." He's got neat rows of tortellini—six, five, four, three, two, one.

I throw the top tortellini at him and it bounces off his forehead.

"You'll regret that, Travers," he says, pelting me with tortellini, two at a time.

"Hey!" I grab a huge handful and fire back.

He keeps coming at me, dodging tortellini before pushing me back to the counter behind me, his hands on either side of me, boxing me in. My smile drops, my breath stuttering out.

He's suddenly so close, the heat of him making my pulse race, my body flushing in excitement.

Then I notice his arm is raised. He's holding the small carton of heavy cream right over my head.

"Don't you dare!" I grab his arm, and he wobbles it threateningly.

"Careful. You're gonna make it spill."

I think quick and grab a nearby wooden spoon, giving his ass a light swat.

He gasps and sets the cream down. "Did you just spank me?"

I laugh. "No."

"Oh, it is on." He wrestles the spoon out of my grip, and I make a run for it, grabbing a throw pillow from his sofa as a shield and running with it against my butt.

He chases me, but I'm nimble and dodge him, running around the coffee table and weaving around a giant recliner. He lunges right, and I go left. Next thing I know we're running in a circle around the coffee table. He fakes a turn, and I run smack into him, drop the pillow, and stumble back over it.

He catches me before I can fall, his arms wrapped around me. His voice is husky, his gaze eating me up. "You're trouble."

I can't help myself. I reach up and stroke his short beard, tracing the line of his strong jaw. He swallows visibly. "You're the one who's trouble."

His big hand cups the back of my neck. Desire pools low in my belly.

A beat passes in shimmering silence before his mouth covers mine. I tilt my head, deepening the kiss. Heat floods me as he takes over the kiss. I'm nearly dizzy with lust and shocked at the intensity.

He breaks the kiss suddenly and pulls away. "I shouldn't have done that."

My stomach drops. "Because of the woman you were with last night?" I blurt.

He stares at the floor for a long moment. "Yeah."

My lips tingle. I can still taste him.

He turns and walks back to the kitchen. "Back to work, party girl."

I follow on shaky legs. The attraction is mutual. My mind whirls for a moment before settling on a hard truth—that's the second time he rejected me. I square my shoulders. I won't let there be a third. Especially knowing he's seeing another woman.

9

———

Brendan

So much for boundaries. I screwed up. I was just messing around with her. Ah, hell. I want her so bad it's impossible to keep my distance for long. I don't know why I'm so into her. Maybe it's because I know she doesn't want serious, so the pressure's off. Somehow that lets her slip in closer than I'd normally allow. I know she's meant for great things, and I'll just be holding her back, but all that seems to go out the window when I'm close to her. Not even family fallout or her psycho ex can put a damper on this thing between us.

I watch as she scoops tortellini in cream sauce onto her plate. Her back is to me while she stands at the stove, so I look my fill. She's petite, her shoulders narrow, her waist narrow, the flare of her hips highlighting a heart-shaped ass in formfitting jeans. I just want to scoop her up and carry her to the bedroom. Something about her size brings out the Neanderthal in me. It's so damn hard not to cross the line.

She looks at me over her shoulder. "Do you want me to scoop some on your plate, or do you want to do it yourself?"

"I got it." I walk around the half-wall counter, where I normally eat. The stools are back in their usual place for our meal.

She passes me, carrying her plate, careful to keep her

distance around me. I know why too. That kiss was electric. It took all of my willpower to step away.

"I'll wait for you so we can try it at the exact same time," she says from her seat at the counter.

"Okay." I scoop a generous helping on my plate and join her. "Ready."

We both stab a piece and take a bite. It's good. Surprisingly good.

"Wow," she says, scooping another tortellini off her plate. "This came out better than I thought from us two cooking newbies. It really makes a difference to make the pasta from scratch."

"Not bad." I take a mouthful of tortellini and chew. I thought Beast was a master chef, but look at us making this awesome meal.

We eat in blissful silence for a few minutes. I can hardly believe I cooked something so tasty. With a little help from Chloe and our pal Massimo. And it only took four hours. Definitely a weekend activity. We should attempt a recipe together every weekend. I stop myself; that's too much time together. Boundaries. Which is exactly why I let her think I was with someone last night. It was easier than explaining my real reason—I'd only hold her back. Besides, now she'll do her part in keeping boundaries too. I know she wants me. She kissed me first back in Villroy. And it's in her eyes, in her breathy voice sometimes, in her flushed cheeks. My gaze catches on the bow in her top lip that I want to trace with my tongue.

I tear my gaze away and take a sip of water. "How's your internship going?"

She rocks her head side to side. "Could be better. I'm doing grunt work basically. I know everyone has to start somewhere, but it's so soul sucking. I'm going to talk to the research director on Monday and broach the topic. I have some credentials to my name. I could be doing so much more."

"Hope it goes well. It can be a touchy thing dealing with bosses." My oldest brother, Dylan, is my boss, and we tangled a bit over my need to take a bigger role in our company once our uncle retired. I was the first of my brothers to speak up, and I play a pivotal role now scouting out development projects. We've got two under our belt with awards for social responsibility and improving neighborhoods. My most recent find didn't work out though. Sucks big time.

"How's your work going?" she asks.

I exhale sharply. "Not great. The property I had my eye on —a lot with low-level warehouses by the waterfront—we lost to a higher bidder looking to make high-rise apartments. My brothers and I don't want to be in that business. We want neighborhoods like the kind we grew up in."

"Sorry."

"Yeah. It sucks because we already had a property there that we developed into cool loft space with a waterfront park. So the plan was to demolish the nearby warehouses and put in upscale co-op apartments with connecting green space and some art installations from our design tenants. It was all gonna be LEED certified environmentally friendly, energy efficient, with reclaimed materials from the area. You know, like wood joists from the old warehouses. Now they're putting in two seventy-story high-rise buildings."

"Seventy stories! That's going to block the view, block out the sun!"

"Right? You lose the neighborhood feel when you're walking between giant skyscrapers. Might as well move to Manhattan for that."

We go back to eating. It's too good to leave it for long.

I finish my plate and go for a second helping. "Anyway, my brothers and I decided we'll be the historic restoration and neighborhood-friendly developer. That'll be our niche."

She shakes her head. "I hope Brooklyn doesn't get overrun by high-rises."

"Right?" I take my seat and dig in. Still fantastic.

"You know, there's an old department store downtown, Finerman's, near where I grew up. I used to like to window-shop there. Anyway, it's been closed for a while now, and I noticed last weekend there's a sale sign on it. Maybe you could turn it into something cool."

"I wonder what they're asking."

"You could look it up online."

"Definitely. Right after this." My pulse thrums through me. This could be something, an old department store. Maybe we could convert it to loft apartments with a rooftop garden. I hadn't realized it was on the market. It must be newly listed. Maybe another transaction fell through behind the scenes.

"Thanks, Chloe. I've got that excited feeling like I'm onto something."

"All atingle? Are you sure it's not crabs?"

I bark out a laugh. She's getting comfortable with me, teasing. "Gross. And no. I've got standards and condoms."

She waves a hand airily. "I don't want to hear about your women."

"Likewise."

She takes a mouthful of tortellini and speaks around it. "I've decided celibacy is the way to go."

"Right."

She chews and swallows. "Seriously."

"We'll see how long that lasts."

She pins me with a hard look. "You a betting man?"

I jerk my chin. "One hundred dollars says you hook up with a guy by the Fourth of July weekend. You'll have off from work, get a little bored, and BAM." She jumps at my BAM, and I stifle a laugh. "Suddenly wimpy lab guy is looking pretty good."

"You're on," she says, offering me her pinky finger.

I wrap my pinky finger around hers, the touch zinging awareness through me. I should stop touching her. Our eyes lock, and her lips part. Everything in me screams to close the distance.

She stands abruptly. "I'll help clean up."

I keep my focus on my plate. I don't need to check her out every time she moves. She's permanently stuck in my brain.

~

Man, I am psyched. My brothers and I are having a Monday lunch meeting at a pizzeria near our latest job. We're doing some work in Queens on a shopping mall. Pays the bills, but it's not what I like best. I like the projects that are developed from the ground up by us, Rourke Management. Is it weird how much I like our name on the company? My whole life I always worked under the Byrne name. Finally, we have something of our own. All of my brothers are here, except Sean, who's still in Vancouver with his wife. We've got him on speakerphone. Me and Beast are on one side of a booth by the front window, Connor and Jack across from us, and Dylan, our CEO, is on a chair at the side.

I wait until everyone's finished their first slice of pizza, letting them take the edge off their hunger before jumping in with my pitch. "I found our next property, the old Finerman's department store. It's historic, from eighteen ninety-three, tons of cool architectural touches you just don't find in modern construction." I pass around the spec sheet my dad gave me. He works in real estate and was able to get me in yesterday to check out the place. I turn to the phone at the center of the table. "Did you get your spec sheet okay, Sean?" I emailed it to him last night.

"Got it."

I continue. "It's seven stories, right downtown, and there's a café next door for sale too. I'm thinking loft apartments, attract some of the hipsters with bucks and a craving for caffeine. We buy the café too. In fact, I'd like to buy up the whole block and make a more cohesive development plan, but that's all we've got available for now."

I'm on the edge of my seat while my brothers look over the specs.

"Elevator?" Dylan asks, lifting tired blue eyes to mine. He's a new dad and says the baby is keen on the four a.m. screaming wake-up call.

"Yes."

"Prewar construction," Connor says with a smile. "Becca would love it. She should be here too." That's his fiancée and our chief strategy officer, which is *not* a partnership position. I have to be firm about this now that my older brothers are mushballs for their women. Seriously, they'll do anything for them. The four of them—Dylan, Connor, Jack, Sean—have to be reminded of blood ties. It's us brothers who are co-owners, whether they're married or engaged.

"She'll get in on it when it's time," I say. "Purchase decisions rest on the owners. Us."

"Josie says it's pretty," Sean says through the phone. "She loved the atrium with the huge skylight when I showed her the specs last night."

I bite my tongue. *Yes, as long as everyone's woman thinks it's "pretty," let's go full steam ahead.*

Jack lifts his head and pushes a lock of dark brown hair out of his eyes. He grows it long on top, styling it with some product that makes him look more hipster than he is. "Lots of convenient subway lines nearby."

"Five-minute commute to downtown Manhattan," I say. "With this square footage, I'm thinking we can get a minimum of one hundred apartments. If we want, we could keep the first two floors as retail space."

"I do like mixed-use development," Dylan says, rubbing his scruffy jaw. "You think they're flexible on price?"

"Only one way to find out," I say with a smile. Triumph rockets through me. If Dylan's on board, the others will fall in place. "We can apply for historic landmark status too. It'll add another credit to that part of our portfolio." Our last project at an old marine rope factory had landmark status too. "And we can still do some of the environmentally friendly, energy-efficient stuff. I think it'll attract high-end tenants."

Dylan leans back in his seat and taps the table. "We should set aside some low-rent space for a nonprofit to work out of. Like one of those groups that tutors disadvantaged kids. It could be a good fit with working professional residential tenants."

We all agree on that point. It's part of our mission to give back to neighborhoods.

Dylan rubs the back of his neck. "I say we make an offer contingent on inspection. Any objections?"

I look around the table. No one seems to object. In fact, Beast is eying his second slice of pizza hungrily.

"Let's go for it," I say.

"I'm in," Sean says through the phone.

My brothers lean toward the phone in a chorus of agreement, letting Sean know where we're at.

"Later," Sean says and disconnects.

Everyone goes back to eating.

"Hey, Bren, did ya scrounge up a date for my wedding?" Jack asks. "Riley needs the final head count." His wedding is three weeks away.

"Nah. You bring a woman to a wedding and she gets the wrong idea."

"Sure?" Jack asks. "We just put Beast here in for a plus one. He invited a girl he met at the music festival this weekend. Major pickup scene."

I arch my brows at Beast.

He shrugs one shoulder. "We hit it off."

Jack takes a long drink of water and points the bottle at me. "You're the only one of us going solo. Maybe I could find someone for you so you don't stick out like a sore thumb when the rest of us are dancing. Can't have you being a wallflower."

My mind flashes to Chloe and her ridiculous dance. And my dance that made her beet red when she realized I was teasing about her solo orgasmic night.

Beast speaks around a mouthful of pizza. "Tara has a best friend who might be willing to go with you."

"Who's Tara?" I ask.

"The girl from this weekend," Beast says. "My date."

"Aren't you worried she'll think it's serious taking her to a wedding?"

"Nope. It's just a date with free food and dancing. She loves dancing." He turns to Jack. "No offense. I'm just talking about her perspective. Of course *I* know it's a major event."

Jack laughs. "No offense taken." He turns to me, his blue eyes dancing with undisguised glee. *Uh-oh.* Jack is *king* of the pranksters. This can't be good.

I gulp. "Whatever you're thinking, no."

Jack holds up a palm. "Hear me out. Mom was telling me—"

"No."

"About a—" he finger quotes "—'nice young woman from church'—"

"Hell no."

Jack goes on unfazed. "She just moved to town. Mom wanted me to introduce her around. I'll introduce her to *you*." He pulls out his phone. "Lemme text Mom right now."

I lunge for his phone, but he leans back out of reach, smiling widely. My brothers chuckle. *Okay, chill.* Maybe this is just a prank and he's texting his fiancée only *pretending* to set me up through our mother. Never underestimate how far Jack will go for a prank. He once spent an entire month carefully trimming the shoelaces of my sneakers on a daily basis until I couldn't tie them. It was so subtle I didn't realize it until the very end. Then I stole his sneakers since we're the same size.

My phone chimes, and I pick it up gingerly. Like it's a lethal cobra about to strike. I tense. *No-o-o.*

Mom: *Brendan, this is wonderful. Her name is Faith. I just know she'll enjoy the wedding at that beautiful church. She's a nice Catholic girl. Okay, now how do I instant flash the contact to you?*

No way I'm helping her with that.

Me: *It's complicated. I'll have to show you in person later.*

Like never.

She accidentally texts a picture of my dad sitting at a restaurant. Then I get a GIF of Snoopy dancing and a series of emojis—surprise face, laughing face, and a heart.

I glare at Jack before typing a quick reply. *Jack was just messing with me. I don't need her number.*

Faith's number and email finally comes through.

Mom: *Did you get it?*

Me: *Yeah, but I'm not calling her.*

Mom: *Bren, it's time you find a nice girl. Faith is wonderful. She's a kindergarten teacher, which means she can put up with the likes of you. Ha-ha.* She adds three sunglasses emojis.

I grind my teeth.

Mom: *I'll have her over for dinner next Sunday. No pressure. Just meet her, okay?*

"How's it going?" Jack asks enthusiastically.

I shoot him the middle finger. The day I date a woman my mother picks out for me is the day hell freezes over. Never surrender!

Me: *I already have a date for the wedding.*

Mom: *You do? Well, what was Jack talking about, then? He said you were the only one without a date.*

Me: *Yanking my chain as usual. He thinks I made her up and had to take matters into his own hands.*

Mom: *I just don't understand the way he thinks. Well, I can't wait to meet her! Love you.*

The tips of my ears burn as I feel my brothers' eyes on me. *Love you too,* I type quickly and put the phone facedown.

"So can I put you down for a plus one?" Jack asks with a smirk.

I press my lips into a flat line. "Yeah. I'm bringing a friend. Not this nice Catholic girl you tried to foist on me. What's the matter with you, pulling Mom into this?" I reach across the table and smack him upside the head.

He laughs.

There's only one woman I can bring to this wedding who won't think it means I'm serious about her. My only woman friend. If Chloe turns me down, I'll never hear the end of the teasing from my brothers. My mother will probably show up with Faith for me. Save me from the matchmaking efforts of moms!

10

Brendan

Be cool. Do *not* act like you care one way or the other. It's Saturday night and I invited Chloe over for pizza and a movie. I planned everything very carefully to look casual. No cooking together. We're watching a comedy, *Monty Python's Holy Grail*. I don't know any woman who would see anything romantic in that movie. Then, at some point, I'll invite her to Jack's wedding as friends. I'll say it's so we can keep an even head count, which is important to Jack's fiancée. Yeah, that should work.

I wipe my sweaty palms on my jeans and pace the living room. She's home. I know she's home, but I'm not going to check on what's taking her so long to get here. She's not late but, hell, I'm right next door. It's fine if she wants to stop by a little early. Maybe I should just get it out of the way right up front. *Chloe, will you go to my brother's wedding as my plus one? Just as friends, of course.*

No, I'd better start with the friends thing. *We're friends and friends can go to weddings together.* I pinch the bridge of my nose. Nope.

Hey, what're you doing two weeks from now? If you answered going to a wedding in New Jersey, you'd be right. Lame.

I pick up one of the throw pillows that came with my sofa,

punch it a few times to fluff it up, and put it back. Then I do the same with the other pillow, placing them on opposite ends of the sofa. That's where we'll sit with a safe friend-zone distance between us.

I flop down on the sofa, lying across the entire thing, and cross my ankles. Maybe I'll just lie here and tell her to come in, so she'll see how chill I am. Of course, I need to unlock the door for that to work.

I roll off the sofa and stride to the door, turning the lock. I'm halfway back to the sofa when there's a soft knock at the door. My heart actually pounds. What is wrong with me? It's just Chloe. Most likely wearing a plain tank top and jeans. Every weekend it's the same outfit, different color, outlining her petite curves. No, her *regular* curves just like every other woman on the planet.

I amble to the door, taking a slow deep breath, ordering my heart to resume normal beating. There is nothing exciting about tonight. No high stakes. I can always go with the girl my mother picked out for me. *Kill me now.*

I open the door and rest both hands casually against the doorframe overhead. "Hey."

Her blond hair is down, resting on her bare shoulders. A white ribbed tank top clings to her perky breasts, the outline of her bra barely visible, faded jeans with frayed edges, white Keds. Exactly as expected. I ignore the tightening in my gut, the lust coursing through my veins. I'm Mr. Casual.

She looks up at me, her brows knitting together over green eyes. "Hi. Uh, are you gonna let me in?"

I draw back, realizing I was blocking the entire space. "What kind of pizza do you like?"

"The only good kind."

"Pepperoni?"

She smiles. "Yup."

How did I know that? It's my favorite. "I'll order it now." I pull my phone from my pocket and tap over to a local place that delivers.

Chloe wanders over to the hideous painting on the living room wall that I can't seem to get rid of. My brother Connor left it behind when he moved out. It's just scribbles in purple and red with a garish yellow dot in the middle. Supposedly it's from a famous artist. I wanted to get rid of it but, even though Connor agreed it was hideous, he said it was a birthday present from our brother Jack, so he had to keep it. I tried to unload it on Connor as a housewarming gift when he moved in with his fiancée, but she says it clashes with her decor. No kidding. It clashes with everything.

"What is this supposed to be?" She tilts her head this way and that. "Close up of a molecule?"

I look at it with new eyes. Problem is, I don't know what a molecule looks like up close. Then I get a great idea. "You like it? It's yours."

She crinkles her nose. "No, thanks."

I go back to ordering pizza. "I'm never getting rid of that thing. Jack gave it to Con as a gift. Con left it behind when he moved out."

"I don't get modern art," she says, taking a seat on the sofa.

"Me either." I place the order. "You want a drink while we wait?"

She shakes her head. "I'm good."

I tuck my phone back in my pocket and consider my next move. She's sitting there, completely oblivious that I'm about to take things to a public level. She's going to hang with my family at Jack's wedding. She knows them a little from Villroy, but this is different. My mom will definitely follow up about her. I think Mom will like Chloe. She's smart, kind, and hardworking. Beautiful. I swallow hard. If Chloe says no to the wedding, I'll have to explain why I'm solo. I refuse to date a nice Catholic girl chosen by my mother. A guy has to draw the line somewhere.

Chloe tucks her hair behind her ears. "Everything okay? You seem tense."

I stride over to the sofa and flop down in a casual gesture. "Perfectly relaxed."

"I was glad to hear your brothers were on board for Finerman's. I always liked that store, even if I couldn't afford anything in it."

We've kept in touch by text. No big. It's what friends do.

"Yeah, we put a bid in, and we're waiting to hear if the owner counters. Fingers crossed." I can't seem to get comfortable. I punch the pillow behind me and push back into it. She's at the opposite end of the sofa with a cushion between us. Just the way me and Beast would sit on this sofa. The center cushion is no-man's land.

She glances over at me and then turns away, twirling a lock of hair. It's awkward, and it shouldn't be. Things were great last weekend when we hung out. There's a comfort level between us that's missing now. It's because of this damn question I have to ask her. *Just spit it out!*

"So, Chloe, I was wondering…" Too wimpy. *Act like you don't care. Like you're asking a guy to the game.*

"Yeah?"

"Ever see Monty Python?" *Dammit.*

"No."

"It's my favorite movie."

She nods. "Cool. I'll pretend I like it, then."

I bark out a laugh. She has a dry deadpan sense of humor that keeps surprising me. "How's work? Are you getting beyond setting up test tubes?"

"Don't forget washing equipment," she says. "I'm the newbie, the youngest in the lab, and I got a nice little lecture from my boss about how everyone has to pull their weight no matter how smart they think they are."

"Ouch."

"Yeah. I swear I wasn't bragging about myself. I just stated plainly what I've accomplished and what I hope to accomplish." She sighs and leans back in the sofa, looking at the ceiling. "I guess I shouldn't have brought my résumé and published papers as a reminder. That seemed to annoy her." She turns her head to look at me. "She said she'd already reviewed them with my application and didn't need to see them again."

"It's tough with bosses. Gotta walk a fine line, respecting

authority while standing up for yourself." I lift a palm. "Look at the bright side. One day you'll be in charge of a lab and you can make some other newbie do crap work."

A reluctant smile tugs at her lips. "I guess someone has to do it."

"My brother Jack's getting married in two weeks," I blurt. "In New Jersey, where his fiancée is from. The reception is at a country club. Real fancy setup."

She nods and kicks off her shoes.

"So what're you doing the Saturday after next?"

She turns to me. "I don't know, Bren. What're we doing?"

My lips curve up. She gave it to me. "We're going to Jack's wedding. As friends."

"Do I have to dance?"

"No."

She inclines her head. "Do you have any popcorn for the movie?"

I'm so relieved I want to hug her. But I can't cross the no-man's land. I know that. She's too tempting, too sexy, too much everything. And she's on a determined path that doesn't include me. I'll never do anything close to as great as being a cancer researcher. Fact is, she's out of my league.

I get off the sofa. "I might have some microwave popcorn somewhere."

"Add extra butter to it. I love too much butter."

I head for the kitchen. "I'll see what I can do."

"Guess who called me earlier."

I open a cabinet, searching for popcorn. "No idea."

"Michael."

I freeze. The guy who proposed to her back in Villroy. "Yeah?" I manage, rummaging around in the cabinet.

"Yeah. He says he's ready to be friends again. He wants to see me when I go back to Villroy in August to visit Sara." She'll be there for a month. My gut does a slow roll.

Friends with benefits? Like before? I don't like that I care so much.

I slam the cabinet closed. "No popcorn."

"Bummer."

I stare at her. "So, are you gonna see him?"

"Yeah. I'm glad he's moved past my rejection. We were good friends before."

I blow out a breath. He wants her back. I know it in my gut.

I walk over to stand in front of her, leaving the coffee table between us. "Do you really think Michael wants to be just friends after everything that went down between you two?"

She blinks in surprise. "That's what he said."

"And you believe him?" I bark.

"Why're you getting so mad?"

I spear a hand through my hair. It's not my business. I know that. I just don't like it. "I'm not mad," I mutter, shifting around to my spot in the furthest corner of the sofa from her.

"You think he's lying?" she asks.

"Yes, Chloe, I think he's lying. No guy wants to go back to being friends after you've had sex with him. And especially after a proposal! It doesn't work that way."

"But..." She trails off at my glare and faces front. "Okay. Thanks for the guy perspective."

"Sure," I grumble.

She grabs the remote control. "Mind if we watch TV while we wait for the pizza?"

"Are you still going to see him in August?"

"He works at the palace. I'm sure we'll run into each other."

Are you going to hook up with him again? I can't ask. I prop my feet on the wooden coffee table and cross my arms, feigning nonchalance as jealousy eats a hole in my stomach.

She flips the channel to a documentary on the wilds of Alaska. I hate documentaries. Look at that dopey brown bear wandering around the stream. Oh, he caught it. Huge fish in his mouth.

We exchange a glance of shared enthusiasm and turn back to the TV. So what if she shows me new things that I actually like? I showed her we could cook. What did Michael ever show her, huh? How to guard something? Useless.

I stew in silence, watching the wildlife, which is more

fascinating than I realized. My phone chimes with a text. The pizza will be here in five minutes.

I stand. "Pizza's almost here. I'm gonna grab a few plates, napkins, and drinks for us, and then I'll head down to meet the pizza guy in the lobby."

"Okay." She digs some money out of her pocket and offers it to me.

"I got it."

"Sure?"

"Put it away. I invited you over, so I can get it."

"Bren, you seem mad again. What's got you so agitated tonight?"

"Look, we're friends, right?"

"Yeah."

"So I'm saying this as a friend. If you see Michael again, he's gonna take that as encouragement. If you don't want to start something again, then you have to keep your distance."

She studies me for a long moment, her eyes searching my face.

I work on looking like a concerned friend. "I'm just giving you the guy perspective."

"Okay, thanks."

She doesn't elaborate. Damn her noncommittal answers. That's my thing.

I lift my palms. "Now you know."

"Do you want me to help set the table or anything?"

"No."

"Okay." She sounds cheerful.

I clench my jaw and stride toward the kitchen. I need to calm the fuck down. I don't have any say in what she does in Villroy. Or here. Or anywhere. She's a free woman. She doesn't even want to dance with me at the wedding. I mean, what if there's a slow dance? She doesn't want to be close to me? She's moved on. So will I. Already did.

I snag plates, napkins, and a glass of water for her. I'll get a beer for myself when I get back with the pizza.

"Are you in the wedding party?" she calls from the sofa.

"No, Jack had too many guys and they had to match up

with the bride's side. My brothers and I drew straws for who'd be a groomsman." I go back to the living room, hand her the water, and set the coffee table for dinner.

"Oh, good."

I lift my gaze to hers. "Why is that good?"

"Because then you'd have a bridesmaid partner you'd have to sit with, and I'd just be sitting by myself. I was maid-of-honor at Sara's wedding and I had to stick with Oscar for a lot of it." That's my cousin, a prince. Most women would've loved to be with Oscar. He was such a player before he met his wife. As bad as I was. Am. I should pick up a woman soon.

"I'm gonna get the pizza." I'm about to head out when she stops me with another question.

"Will we be spending the night in New Jersey after the wedding?"

I halt. It's about a two-hour drive. *Does she want to spend the night with me?* There is a breakfast the next morning at my new sister-in-law's parents' house. It's optional, though. I rented a car so I could come and go as I please, depending how I felt after the wedding.

I slowly turn back, my pulse thrumming in anticipation. "We could go either way, spend the night or come back. Which do you prefer?"

She bites her lip and looks away. "Whatever works for your family. I was just wondering."

Which is the most confusing answer I've ever heard.

"They'd probably like to see me at the breakfast the next day, so we'll spend the night." I wait, gauging her reaction.

"Great," she says tightly.

Guess I know where I stand. She looks uncomfortable with the idea. Whatever. I really don't care. She can go back to her long-distance arrangement with Michael, and I'll just…I'll just deal.

I yank open the front door and stalk out. Pizza and a movie. That's it.

I get the pizza, tip the guy, and head back upstairs, deter-mined to get back on solid ground. Enough of this stupid hoping for something more. There's plenty of women out there who'd love to be with a guy like me.

I burst through the door, startling her. "We're not spending the night."

"Okay," she says, her voice going up at the end like a question. Her brows draw down as she studies me. "What is with you tonight?"

"Nothing. I just think it's better if we don't drag out the weekend any more than we absolutely have to. Weddings are exhausting." I stalk to the coffee table and deposit the pizza box.

"Bren, do you not want me to go to Jack's wedding? Would you rather go alone? I totally get that."

"I asked you; you said yes." I lift the lid of the box. "Eat up."

She salutes me. "Yes, sir!"

A laugh escapes and I join her, taking a slice for myself. "Smart-ass."

She smiles. "Can't help it."

"Yeah, me neither."

"Does watching your brothers get married make you want that too?" she asks before taking a big bite of pizza.

I open my mouth to say no, but what comes out is, "Someday." Huh. Maybe I am evolving. My older brothers are happier than I've ever seen them before. It could be rubbing off on me.

She nods and takes a swig of water. "Yeah, when I see Sara with baby Henry, I think someday I'd like to be a mom."

"Not a wife?"

She lifts a shoulder. "Guess the guy goes with the territory." She pulls a funny face, twisting her lips. "Such a hassle with all their testosterone and demands."

"Ha! What about all the hormones women are riding? Up and down with the moods. God help ya if you catch them at the wrong time of the month."

"Sexist."

"So are you."

She sighs. "Sometimes I wish I were a lesbian. So much simpler."

"Even better would be if you met a lesbian fellow doctor."

She takes a bite of pizza, speaking around it. "Too bad I like dick so much."

"Yeah," I croak. Thank God I didn't get my beer yet, or I'd be spewing it now. As it is, my cock twitched to life at her crude language. She might look angelic, but she's not shy. She once told me she had no inhibitions in bed. That is the stuff of my lusty dreams.

I close my eyes for a second, telling my cock to stand down. *Icy wind, moldy onions, dates set up by my mother.* There. Better.

"I'm gonna get a beer," I say.

I keep my head in the refrigerator extra long just for the cold air.

11

———

Chloe

It's strange how quickly I've gotten close to Brendan. We're driving to a church in northern New Jersey on a beautiful sunny day, the last weekend in June, rock music blasting. Usually my relationships with guys tend to be off and on to satisfy mutual physical needs mostly. It's been a month since I moved in next door to him, and I have to admit he's awesome. I look forward to hanging with him every weekend, even if we're just taking a walk or grabbing a pizza. He's the first person I want to share about my day and the last person I want to talk to at night. We have an open-door policy, popping into each other's apartments any time and texting frequently. And to think it wouldn't have happened if I hadn't moved here for my internship.

I glance over at him in profile as he drives, his features dear to me now, the faint scar by his eyebrow, his sharp cheekbones, and short beard. He looks so handsome in his gray suit. Every time I'm tempted to cross the line, which is often, I remind myself he's got another woman. It could be multiple women for all I know. I swallow hard, my gut churning, and look away. I have no right to be hurt, but I can't help it. We're close in so many ways. It's hard knowing he stays out all night every Friday night. *Stop it. He invited you to this wedding, not any other woman, because he likes to spend time with you most of all.* There's definitely an advantage to being a close friend instead of one of many casual—nope, not going there.

He turns into the church lot and parks. "This is it. Ready?"

"Ready." I grab my small purse and open the door, careful to get out of the car without flashing anyone. I'm wearing a teal spaghetti-strap cocktail dress with a V-neck, the material gathered in diagonal pleats in the bodice that makes it look like I have more curves up top than I do. My sister made sure I had dresses for a variety of occasions once she became co-owner of the casino in Villroy. We went shopping at some of the best boutiques in Paris. The clothes seem made for a petite size like mine.

Brendan appears at my side, shutting the car door behind me. "I should've opened that for you."

I cock my head. "I'm perfectly capable of opening a door."

He leans close. "Yeah, but you're my date. Just friends, but still. My dad is a stickler for manners, and he'll notice if I'm not pouring on all the gentlemanly etiquette or whatever."

Weird but okay.

He offers me his arm, and I stare at it. He takes my hand and rests it on his forearm; then he starts walking toward the church. I'm suddenly intensely aware of him, the heat of his arm through his gray blazer, the hard muscle, his woodsy sexy scent. I swallow hard and stare straight ahead.

"I bet ya Jack pulls a prank today," he says.

"On his wedding day?"

He laughs. "Any day, but especially one when you least expect it."

"If I were the bride, I'd be pissed."

"She's just as bad. They're constantly pranking each other."

"Then I guess they're well matched."

"No one else could put up with him," he says with a laugh.

As soon as we step into the front of the church, two groomsmen in black tuxes offer us a program. They're his brothers—same dark brown hair and sky blue eyes—though I can't remember which is which since the resemblance is so strong. Beast is easy to pick out with his huge muscles. And Dylan, the oldest, stands out just from the way he carries himself. The other three are a blur of dark brown hair, sharp cheekbones, and various amounts of scruff.

"Sean, you made it," Brendan says, giving one of the ushers a bro hug and a slap on the back.

"Got in around midnight," Sean says, smiling. His hair is cut short and he's got just enough stubble to make a dark shadow on his jaw. "Couldn't miss Jack's big day. I'm heading back tomorrow. Unfortunately, Josie couldn't get away, her schedule leaked into the weekend. Sometimes that's the way it goes with union hours."

Brendan introduces us, reminding his brothers of my connection to the family, and catches me up on them. "Josie's his actress wife. She's filming a movie."

Connor—his dark brown hair long on top, scruff almost to beard territory—regards Brendan with a quizzical look. "Bride or groom?"

"Yes," Brendan says, giving Connor's arm a friendly smack.

Connor gestures around his head. "Chloe, didn't you have red hair at the Christmas ball in Villroy?"

"Yes, just a temporary thing."

Sean stares at me. "That's right. Bren wanted to ask you to dance." He lifts his brows. "Guess that worked out."

"Oh, no, we're just friends," I say immediately.

"Yeah, friends," Brendan echoes.

I catch him making a slashing motion across his throat to his brothers out of the corner of my eye.

Connor's lips twitch. "Always nice to meet a friend of Brendan's." He hands me a program and gestures to the right. "Groom's side is over there."

Brendan guides me down the aisle, his hand resting on the small of my back, heating my skin through the thin fabric of my dress. Considering he invited me as a friend, he's already touched me more today than he has in the past month. Except for that one scorching hot kiss the night we made tortellini. I like to pretend that was just a dream.

He guides me into the second row, where Dylan is already seated with his wife, holding their adorable baby girl. My heart squeezes. The baby is in a white bonnet with a light pink rosebud pattern and matching dress. I smile at her, and she beams back a smile, two little white baby teeth appearing on the bottom. *Awww!*

Brendan makes the introductions. It's Dylan, Ariana, and baby Olivia. I'm enthralled with this happy baby. As soon as I sit down next to Ariana, Olivia reaches toward me and pats my cheek with her pudgy baby hand.

"Aren't you a cutie?" I coo. "Do you like peekaboo?" I cover my face with a hand and peek between my fingers. She stares in concentration. I drop my hand and smile. "Peeka-boo!" She squeals and bounces in her mom's arms.

Ariana smiles at me, her dark brown eyes kind. "You're a natural."

"I know how to entertain a baby," I say, covering my face again. "I have a baby nephew." I pop out with my peekaboo, and Olivia giggles madly. "I love babies."

Ariana leans forward. "Did ya hear that, Bren? Sounds promising."

I stiffen and glance toward Brendan, who doesn't look nearly as alarmed as I feel. Strange. I turn back to Ariana. "We're just friends. Really good friends."

"That's nice," she murmurs, exchanging a look with her husband sitting on her other side.

They don't believe me. I turn to Brendan, and my hair is suddenly yanked painfully hard. *Ow!* I gasp and reach back to hold my hair in place. The baby's got a hold of me.

"I'm so sorry," Ariana says, working on getting the baby's fingers free. "She's fascinated with blond hair. Most of us are brunettes." The baby yanks my hair up and down until her dad gets a hold of her arm while her mom works on loos-ening her fingers. *Babies don't know their own strength.* "She does the same thing to Connor's blonde fiancée."

I catch Brendan fighting a laugh. I narrow my eyes, and he laughs out loud.

His parents—I remember them from Villroy—take the first row, sitting right in front of us. They're probably in their late fifties and seem very close. Mrs. Rourke turns to smile at us and then frowns. "Olivia, we have got to get you a blond dolly, so you stop accosting blonde women. Let go, sweetheart."

"It's okay," I say on a wince.

Finally, the baby's grip is free. Mrs. Rourke holds out her arms for her granddaughter, and Ariana passes her over. Mrs. Rourke bounces her a little. "You look familiar," she says to me with a smile, her blue eyes sparkling just like Brendan's. "Have we met?"

"Villroy," Mr. Rourke says. "I remember. Prince Adrian's wife's sister. How lovely to see you on this special occasion."

"Thank you," I say. "Nice to see you again."

"This is Chloe Travers, future doctor," Brendan says. "She moved into the apartment next door, and we've been hanging out ever since."

"A doctor?" Mrs. Rourke asks with enthusiasm, her smile bright. "Wow. What kind?"

"My goal is to become a cancer researcher," I say.

His parents stare at me with twin expressions of surprise.

"She's a genius," Brendan puts in. "She's finishing under-grad at Columbia in only three years."

My cheeks heat. "I'm not a genius." Brendan's always saying that. It takes more than smarts to do what I've done. It's all about work ethic. I work my ass off during the school year. I'm learning to take time off when school's out.

"That's wonderful," Mrs. Rourke says. "What a noble cause."

Mr. Rourke arches a brow. "So what do you see in this guy?" He ruffles Brendan's hair, whose ears and neck turn bright red. "I kid because I love, Chloe. You'll see." He winks at me.

Brendan smooths his hair, scowling. His parents turn

around as the groom and his ushers appear at the front of the church.

I lean close to whisper in Brendan's ear, "I see where you get your teasing side from."

"It's a family trait," he grumbles. "You can never escape it."

"I get the feeling you dish out more than your fair share."

He takes my hand and gives it a squeeze, his mouth tilting up on one side, revealing his dimple. He trimmed his beard, which makes his adorable dimple more noticeable. I wish I were immune to his charms. "You know me so well."

And now we're holding hands.

I stare straight ahead, flushed with heat over the simplest, most innocent of touches.

The ceremony is a blur, though I try hard to focus. I want to see if Jack or Riley pull a prank. All my senses are tuned into the man next to me, his large hand enveloping my smaller one in a warm firm grip. I'm both on edge and comforted by his touch. Is this what it's like when your best friend morphs into a boyfriend? And who said he could do that? What about his Friday night women?

Jack lifts the bride's veil and sets it back over her head. Tears stream down her cheeks. He frames her face with both hands for a timeless moment that brings a lump to my throat. I can't see his face. *Is he crying too?* Why do people cry at weddings? It's a happy occasion.

Brendan gives my hand a squeeze, and I find myself leaning against his side.

A few minutes later, they're pronounced husband and wife. Everyone applauds and Brendan whistles loudly. The happy couple heads down the aisle together. The bride's dress has a long train, which she hooks over one arm as she walks, smiling at everyone, no tears in sight. *That's better.*

Brendan guides me out into the aisle with the crowd slowly following the happy couple. He sticks close behind me, his heat at my back. Our personal boundary bubble seems to have disappeared. But it's a family wedding. How much trouble could we get into here? It's not like we're going to hook up at the country club reception.

He whispers in my ear, and a hot shiver races down my spine. "I never thought Jack would get hitched. He never stuck with anyone before her. I mean *never*."

I glance back over my shoulder at him. "Have you ever stuck?"

He grins down at me. "Nope."

I face front. He's definitely hooking up with multiple women on Friday nights. I swallow down bile. I can't let myself think about that.

Everyone lines up on the path in front of the church to congratulate the bride and groom. After we congratulate them, Brendan pulls me toward the front of the line and says under his breath, "Didn't I tell you there'd be a prank?"

"Now?" I ask, looking around.

Sean and Connor gesture us over by the corner of the church. People are gradually filtering back behind the building. Interesting.

Once we get there, Connor hands me an odd item. It looks like an inflatable brick. "We're throwing this at them instead of bird seed."

Sean nods. "Wait until they're about to get in the limo for the ride to the reception. We'll all throw on the best man's cue. That's Sam." He points out a guy standing on the church steps.

We go back in place and wait. "How is this appropriate?" I ask Brendan, holding the brick behind my back. His family is really weird in a fun way. I like it.

"Tell ya later," he says. "Act casual."

"So this wasn't the bride's or groom's idea?"

"It was Sam's idea to prank the pranksters. He's Riley's brother and Jack's best friend."

I wait and watch. Brendan's family keeps exchanging looks and smiles. The love is so obvious, like a living, breathing thing connecting them all. A stab of envy goes through me. He has no idea how lucky he is.

He elbows me with a grin. "Get ready."

"Bride and groom, front and center," Sam booms. "Get ready for your send-off!"

Jack and Riley go to the top of the steps and wave at all of us, smiling radiantly. Everyone gathers close near the front steps and in a line down the sidewalk.

"Here they are, Mr. and Mrs. Walsh-Rourke!" Sam announces, gesturing at them and nodding at us. *The signal!*

Riley laughs, and they head down the steps as we throw inflatable bricks at them. They both grab one as a souvenir. On one side, in silver block letters it says Walsh-Rourke. They hurry down the path to the limo as bricks bounce off them.

I turn to find Brendan laughing with his brothers and Sam, thrilled with their prank.

I catch his eye and he walks over to me, pulling me aside from the crowd. "You probably think we're nuts pelting the bride and groom with bricks."

"No-o-o."

He arches his brows in a skeptical look. "Yeah."

"Okay, yeah. What's the deal?"

"Once upon a time, Jack and Riley almost weren't. No, wait, first Jack gave her an engraved brick for her birthday when they were secretly married but no one knew. Long story short, it wasn't a real marriage. Then, in a big romantic gesture, Riley had the engraving changed to Walsh-Rourke, letting Jack know she wanted to marry him for real, forever and ever, amen."

I smile. "That's cool."

He kisses my temple. "I knew you'd get it."

I cover my surprise at the unexpected kiss with a cheery smile. "Time for the reception."

His hand rests on my lower back, guiding me through the parking lot to his rental car. "So, I'm just gonna let you know right now you don't *have* to dance with me."

"I know."

"But I want you to." He steps away, doing a waltz with an invisible partner as cars are zigzagging all over the lot to multiple exits.

Careful!

I run up to him and grab him by the shoulders. "You're gonna get hit by a car, crazy man."

He drops an arm over my shoulders and walks toward our car again. "Good thing I've got you."

His arm around me feels so natural, as if we're an actual couple. I allow myself to pretend we are. Just for today.

12

———

Brendan

Dinner's over, and I'm sitting at our table, waiting for Chloe to get back from the ladies' room. The country club is fancy with white columns out front, plenty of chandeliers inside, along with glossy hardwood flooring. I don't even recognize half the people here. Bunch of oldies. I figure they're Riley's parents' friends, all members of the country club. Her family must be loaded. Not my style, but Jack looks right at home chatting with her parents over by the head table. Good for him.

I glance around my table, where the non-groomsmen brothers are sitting. It's me, Beast, and Dylan. Plus Beast's date—he seems into her—and Dylan's wife, Ariana, and their baby. They brought a high chair over for baby Olivia. She's not eating, just playing around with a rattle and squishy turtle. My parents are sitting with us too, but they went off to mingle.

Someone takes Chloe's seat, and I'm about to say the seat's taken when I realize it's my mom. "Hey, boo," she says in a playful tone.

Sounds like she's had a few glasses of champagne.

"Hey, you." My mom's fifty-eight, but could pass for younger. Her fair skin has only a few lines, her shoulder-length dark brown hair has zero gray in it, and she has a lot of energy. She'd have to be high energy to keep six mischievous boys in line. I was the most mischievous, but Jack was a close second with his pranks.

She beams and squeezes my shoulder. "Where's your date?"

"She'll be back. Just stopped in the restroom."

"I like her. Smart, serious, a doctor!"

"Yeah, that's her."

"Still, I worry you're leading her on. She's what, twenty-one?"

"Twenty," I mumble.

"Yeah, so when a twenty-year-old dates an older man, they might be expecting something a little more serious."

I shake my head. "It's not like that. We're just friends."

She smacks my shoulder. "Good one."

"No, really. Ask her yourself."

Her brows draw down. "Oh. The champagne must've dulled my mom radar."

Beast pipes up from my other side. "He's hoping to get out of the friend zone, but he doesn't know how. Two words, bro: slow dance." He gestures toward the dance floor.

His new girlfriend, Tara, smiles and rubs his chest. He places a hand over hers.

I glare at him. Like I need women advice from my little brother. "I'm not stuck in the friend zone. We *want* to be friends. She's going off to med school with a lot of training ahead of her." *She's a genius, destined for great things. And I'm not.*

Sitting here surrounded by all these loving couples sucks. I'm beginning to think love is never going to happen for me. And the stupidest thing is, I never wanted that before, and now I'm jealous I don't have it. It must be the wedding putting these ridiculous ideas in my head.

"Shh, shh," Mom says, suddenly sitting straight. Like when the teacher shows up after leaving the kids to their own devices in the classroom. Caught! She's definitely had her share of champagne.

I slowly turn around.

Chloe is standing there, looking from me to my mom to Beast. "Were you talking about me?" she asks in a small voice.

My mom stands and squeezes her arm. "Just saying good things, sweetie." She looks around for my dad and makes a beeline to him. He wraps an arm around her shoulders while they talk to the other oldies.

Chloe takes her seat, tucks her hair behind her ears, and stares at the table, looking extremely uncomfortable.

I lean close. "She was just curious about us. I said we were friends."

She nods, still staring at the table.

Ariana waves across the table at us. "Hey, Chloe, would you like to hold Olivia? She's been dying to play peekaboo with you again."

"I'd love to," Chloe says and heads over there. The moment the baby's in her arms, she relaxes, cooing at her. I don't know what it is about babies that brings out this warm, loving side in her. I only know I long to see more of it.

Chloe's sitting next to me again at our table and seems relaxed after hanging with Ariana and the baby. The bridal party is dancing to a slow song, and I really want to slow dance with Chloe. I just want an excuse to touch her that won't get me in trouble. It's not like we'd ever make out on a dance floor surrounded by family and friends.

Chloe turns to me. "You think there'll be any more pranks tonight?"

I lean back in my chair and look over at Jack and Riley on the dance floor. "Guarantee it. Though I'm not sure if it'll be public. Jack might prank her on their wedding night."

She crinkles her nose. "That's just wrong. That should be your special romantic night, hearts and flowers stuff, don't you think?"

"You're missing the most important part."

Her head whips toward mine, her eyes widening. "Bren."

"What?"

"Don't talk dirty to me." She outlines a circle around herself. "Personal boundary bubble."

I lift my palms. "I didn't talk dirty. You filled in the blank."

She nudges my shoulder with hers. "Besides, I don't want to think about your brother fucking."

Beast chuckles on my other side, and I realize her voice carried. I lower my voice, hoping she'll do the same. Since we're talking dirty, I keep it up. "Who do you like to think about fucking?"

"Blaze."

I stiffen. I didn't actually expect her to answer. "Ah, yes, good ol' Blaze." Who the hell is this Blaze guy? How come I've never seen him stop by? He's probably a genius guy from the lab where she works. I hope he wears a pocket protector and has scrawny arms.

I study her, waiting for more information. The woman is a vault, casually sipping iced water and watching the couples dancing.

I speak through my teeth. "Does Blaze have a last name?"

Her green eyes dance with amusement. "I never asked him."

"So it's pretty casual."

She bites her lower lip, fighting a smile. "No strings."

She's got to be messing with me. "You made him up."

"No, I didn't. Blaze exists, and we meet up regularly."

A stab of pure jealousy has me sitting straighter. "How come I never heard about him before?"

She lifts one shoulder in a careless shrug. "I didn't think we shared stuff like that with each other."

"Well, we could."

She gets serious. "I don't want to hear the nitty-gritty on your Friday night hookups, so let's just leave it there, okay?"

I work my jaw, trying to decide how to play this. I really need to know what's up with this Blaze guy. On the other hand, I've been playing it like I meet a woman on Friday nights when I stay out all night. She'll be mad that I lied, even though it's for her own good. It's so much easier not to cross the line when she keeps her distance.

The DJ announces, "Would everyone please join the bridal party for this next slo-o-ow dance? Come on, now, don't be shy."

One by one, my brothers get up from our table, bringing their dates with them. My parents were already near the dance floor, taking pictures, so they join in too. Even baby Olivia is up there, tucked in the crook of Dylan's arm while he dances with his wife. Our table is now empty except for me and Chloe.

Last man standing.

I lean close to her ear and drop my voice to a husky tone. "Every one of my brothers is on the dance floor with their dates."

She turns, so close I feel her sharp intake of breath. "You said I didn't have to dance."

I tilt my head. "Don't make me look like a wiener." It's one of her favorite expressions. *Wiener.* She's funny in her own weird way.

She looks at me under her lashes. "I like wieners."

I laugh, take her hand, and draw her up. "Come on, you can handle one slow dance."

She follows me without a word, her hand tucked in mine.

Once we're on the dance floor, I rest my hands on her hips. I could do a waltz with some space between us, but that's not what I want. Her arms go around my neck a moment later, and I almost sigh in relief. We sway in time to the music while I breathe in her sweet flowery scent. She's quiet, looking at a point over my shoulder, and I'm not sure where her head's at.

"What do you like so much about babies?" I ask.

She brightens, meeting my eyes. "They're so sweet, and they smell so good. Fresh and new. Plus they need you so much. No one ever needed me for anything."

I consider that. She's the younger sister, so Sara took care of her.

"Didn't you ever take care of a doll or a pet or something?"

She rolls her eyes. "We couldn't have pets at our apartment and a doll isn't the same. I guess you could say I take care of myself, but that's not nearly as fun as taking care of a little one."

"Well, you've done a fine job taking care of Kablooey." That's her good luck troll.

She laughs. "I guess so."

I pull her closer, my hand resting on the small of her back. She doesn't pull away. In fact, she seems to melt against me. I can't hold back much longer. I feel too much, want too much. We don't talk, yet somehow our bodies seem to be speaking their own language. Her soft curves press against me, and the heat builds between us.

The song changes to a fast one, and Chloe pulls away.

"Not my thing," she says in a breathy voice, heading back to our table.

I don't push it. I give her space and join Jack with his friends at the center of the dance floor. He throws an arm over my shoulders and grins at me. I wish I could be as happy as he is. All these weddings, watching my older brothers get hitched, happier than they've ever been, it's made an impression on me. Makes me think maybe there is something worthwhile in sticking around.

I glance over at Chloe reading something on her phone. Probably the latest genetic research. She's so different from me, but in a lot of ways we seem to fit. I don't know how it would work out for us long term with her going off to med school and me being anchored here, but we have now. Isn't it worth trying?

∼

Chloe

Things got a little dicey on the dance floor with Bren. Being held in his arms, it felt like something real between us. Yet I can't ignore the fact that he's out with other women. I don't believe he sees me as a conquest; we truly are friends. But there's an undeniable chemistry that we've both tiptoed around. The whole thing just makes me sad and confused. I don't have a lot of close friends like Bren in my life. It feels like we're inching toward shaky ground, and I don't want to lose him.

The moment he returns to the table, flushed from his exertion on the dance floor, I say, "I don't think we should slow dance again."

He taps the end of my nose and gets in my face. "I don't remember asking." He flops down in his seat and takes off his blazer, setting it on the back. Then he loosens his tie and undoes the top two buttons of his white dress shirt, revealing his sexy chest.

I face front. *Nice, Chloe, checking him out while you sit here worried about losing his friendship.* I don't think I've ever been this confused where a guy's concerned.

Brendan leans back in his chair, spreading his knees and resting his arm across the back of my chair. Is he making a move on me, or is he man spreading? I guess you could say I don't have a good handle on the male species. I should read up on their psyche, really figure this stuff out. If I turn it into a scientific exploration, maybe I'll be less confused.

The rest of the reception goes by relatively smoothly. Brendan and I talk a lot, and he takes me around, introducing me to people in his family. I do the requisite small talk, but all I can focus on is Bren's palm at the small of my back or his smile or his hand holding mine. His touch is casual, reassuring, and I'm starting to crave it.

We get back to Brooklyn late that night. I fell asleep in the car, so I'm groggy when we walk back to our building, but the moment we reach my door, I wake up. He's quiet, but there's a comfortable intimacy between us after spending hours together talking, touching, *craving.*

He looks down at me, his blue eyes intent on mine, his expression serious. "Thanks for going with me."

"I had a good time."

He gazes into my eyes, and all I can think about is the classic end-of-date goodnight kiss. But this was a friends date, right? Right?

I thrust my hand out to shake. He stares at it for a long moment, making no move to follow suit. I turn it into a little farewell wave, my cheeks hot.

He takes my hand and brushes his lips across my knuckles, his eyes half hooded. A tingle runs up my arm, my stomach flip-flopping.

"Bren," I say on a shaky note. He's still holding my hand.

His voice is husky, his gaze hungry. "Yeah?"

I need to stay strong, to hang on to what we have, especially knowing he hasn't been longing for me the way I've been longing for him. He's been with other women. "We have boundaries for a reason. I only have a month left on my internship before I leave for Villroy, and then I'm back to school."

He drops my hand. "You're gonna see your guard in Villroy, aren't you?"

"Yes, we're friends."

He scowls. "I know *exactly* what kind of friend arrangement you had with him."

"It's not like that anymore."

"He's not over you, Chloe. If he felt strongly enough to propose, I can guarantee he's gonna try to win you back."

"You don't have to be jealous. I can have guy friends. Like you and me."

He clenches his jaw and bites out, "Not even close."

I swallow hard. Brendan is never mad at me. Things are about to go downhill between us despite my best efforts. The thought makes it hard to breathe, a panicky feeling making me desperate to fix it.

He backs away, his voice harsh. "Goodnight, Chloe." He turns and stalks to his apartment next door.

"Wait, Bren!" I close the distance. "I have no plans to go back to friends with benefits with Michael. He might take it as encouragement that we have a future. We don't. I'm staying in the US long term, and he's staying in Villroy, okay?"

He crosses his arms and studies me for a long moment. "Why're you telling me this?"

"I just don't want you to be upset." I wring my hands

together. "It's over between me and Michael. In fact, he mailed back the stuff I left at his place. But if I see him in Villroy, which I'm sure I will since he works at the palace, I'm not going to give him the cold shoulder. I don't want to hurt anyone."

He uncrosses his arms, relaxing a little, though he still seems mad at me. "And what about Blaze, huh?"

My cheeks flush, and I go on the defensive. "What about the fact that you regularly stay out all night hooking up with random women?"

We have a staredown. His hookups are much worse than me using Blaze. My outrage must shine through because I win.

He throws his hands up. "I lied, okay? There. I said it."

I blink a few times, my mind rearranging what I thought was reality. "But—"

He runs a hand through his hair, rumpling it. "I *wish* I could stop thinking about you long enough to even give someone else a second look!"

I suck in air.

He plants his hands on his hips. "I crash at a friend's place in the city after a late night. That's it." He slices a hand through the air. "Me and Stewie. My hot date."

"Oh." My heart's in my throat, adrenaline racing through me. "Blaze isn't a guy. It's what I call my vibrator."

A smile tugs at his lips as he shakes his head. "You got me on that one." He exhales sharply. "So where does that leave us?"

I break into a cold sweat. "I don't know."

He steps closer. "Chloe, tell me you feel something for me."

I bite my lower lip. This thing between us is deeper than anything I've ever felt before, and I'm unexpectedly terrified. Everyone close to me has been ripped away. First my parents, then my sister when she moved to Villroy to be with Adrian. I had to give Sara her freedom; she deserved it. Didn't mean it hurt any less. I'm always the one left behind. I can't risk it.

My gut churns, sweat running down my spine. "Bren,

you're important to me. I want you to stay in my life, and—" I practically choke on the words, unable to make eye contact "—friends last longer than lovers."

He pinches my chin, forcing me to meet his eyes. "I'm talking about a relationship."

"I can't," I say softly.

He drops his hold on me and goes into his apartment without another word.

I stare at his closed door for a moment, my eyes hot before turning to my apartment. I let myself in, heading straight to the bedroom. I drop my purse on the nightstand and flop backward into bed, throwing an arm over my stinging eyes. Is our friendship over forever just because I don't want what he wants? Doesn't he understand how risky it is to let deep feelings in? It can destroy you. I never let anyone in that close.

I sniffle and sit up, wanting to call Sara, but then I realize it's the middle of the night in Villroy. I can't wake her, especially when baby Henry is still getting up at night regularly. It's even late in Texas, so I can't call my friend Lindsey either. The only friend I know is awake is the one person who left me in this agitated state.

I'll let him cool off and try to talk to him tomorrow. I'm not letting our friendship go so easily. I can't lose him.

13

Brendan

The next morning I go for a run first thing. I pushed Chloe for more and her answer was clear—hell no. She's not ready for a relationship, and I, of all people, being king of the casual hookup, really can't take it personally. She's just not in the same place in her life as I am. She's young with lots of work ahead of her, a long arduous journey to becoming a medical researcher. You know, it snuck up on me, but I'm finally ready for a serious relationship. Would you look at that? I'm growing. I head for a nearby park, doing a mental roll call of the women I've met who might be worth a call. There could be some potential there I never took the time to explore.

I start at a slow jog. There was that brunette with the piercings. What was her name? Or maybe that redhead—

Chloe at the Christmas ball.

No, don't think of her.

Soft blond hair, green eyes, smooth flawless skin, those lips with the bow in the top. Fuck. *Get out of my head, Chloe.*

I run faster, but it's no use. It's Chloe my mind returns to again and again. What am I supposed to do about her? She's here for another month, and then she'll be heading to Villroy, where her ex will be waiting. She says she's not getting back with Michael, but I'm sure he's going to try to get with her.

Who wouldn't? She's amazing, beautiful, brilliant, funny, sexy. Ugh. I'm never going to get her out of my head.

I run faster and faster until I can't think of a thing but my next step, my next breath. If only I could keep up the pace.

I slow it down after a while, but then a surprising thing happens as I catch my breath, a peace comes over me. I'm not going to fight it anymore. I'm falling for her and that means I'm going to spend whatever time I can with her, whether or not we ever cross the line into the bedroom. I just want to be with her. Maybe it'll happen for us down the line, when she's ready. I shouldn't push her so much.

I walk toward home, drenched in sweat and fatigued. New plan—be chill. I'm not going to put a label on it, not going to insist we do anything more than what we've been doing. Jack's wedding got me thinking of more, but it shouldn't have. I'm not Jack, after all.

All I know for sure is I'm not going to waste this last month with her. I'll take her any way I can get her. That's not as pathetic as it sounds, I reassure myself. It's called opening my eyes to the amazing woman next door and appreciating her just as she is.

Once I get back home, I take a shower and decide to clear the air with Chloe. I'll see if she wants to do something neutral, like Frisbee in the park. No big if she says no. I know her work is important to her. I'm sure she's home. She's always home on Sunday mornings, though it's creeping close to noon.

After my shower, I head over to her apartment just as she's coming out the door, holding a large plastic container. She freezes, standing in her doorway, staring up at me.

"Hey, I was just going to see…" I trail off. "Where are you going?"

She smiles uncertainly. "I, uh, made you sugar cookies." She holds the container up.

I stare at the cookies. "You did?" No woman has ever baked for me before. I know what this means to her. Sugar cookies are how she gives from the heart. She's talked about making these with Sara, growing up, with warm nostalgia.

She does have feelings for me. There's hope. A surge of affection rushes through me, my limbs suddenly light.

I lift my head and smile. "Thank you."

She lets out a breath, her eyes watering. "You're welcome." She backs up so I can come in.

I take the container from her with one hand and give her a one-armed hug with the other. "You okay?"

She nods, her lips pressed tightly together like she's trying not to cry. "Yeah."

I lift the container. "Why?"

She stares at my chest. "I felt like things got off track last night, and I was really hoping we could still be friends. I don't want to lose you in my life." Her voice chokes with emotion. I must mean a lot to her. That's all I need to know. I don't know how this is going to work, or if it will work, but what we have is real and that's enough.

She's tense, worrying her lower lip. It occurs to me that she might just be scared because she's new to the relationship thing. My protective instinct comes out, wanting to reassure her.

I dip my head, meeting her eyes. "Hey, it's fine. You didn't have to do this." I lift the clear container and peer inside. There's layers and layers of tiny cookies. "What are they supposed to be?"

"Oh." She laughs and takes the lid off the container. "I couldn't find any cookie cutters in the cabinet, but there were these little leaf pie cutters. You know, to decorate a pie with." She takes out a tiny leaf cookie. "You use these on pie dough and decorate the top of it with them. It made so many." That must've taken hours to cut and bake all those tiny cookies. All for me.

I try one. "Very good."

She smiles. "I'm glad you like it."

"Help yourself."

She takes one too, but she doesn't eat it. "So can we hang out today?" She sounds hesitant, like I might turn her down. Was I that harsh last night, or is she just that worried about losing me?

"Absolutely. It's nice out. I was thinking Frisbee in the park. We could grab a bite to eat while we're out. Unless you need to study."

She lifts her chin, her green eyes sparkling. "I've decided to take weekends off in the summer." She pops the cookie in her mouth.

"Really? The whole weekend? Are you sure the research articles won't pile up unread, Dr. Travers?"

She smiles, shaking her head. "A wise man once told me that scientists make the best discoveries when they take regular breaks." That would be me. For completely selfish reasons.

"What? He sounds like a guy who wastes his time."

"No, you were right. I need it, or I'll burn out before I reach my goal."

"So I'm wise, eh? Never been accused of that before."

We smile at each other for a long moment. I think she's as happy as I am that we're hanging out again.

I snap to attention. "Right. So let me put these cookies back at my place and get my Frisbee."

"Great. I'll meet you in a few. I need to get my sunscreen and a hat."

I turn to go and then stop, turning back to her. "What're you doing on the Fourth of July?" It's this Thursday and I have off work for the long weekend.

"I don't know. What're we doing?"

I grin. "You're going to my family's Fourth of July barbecue. My dad makes a big deal ever since he became an American citizen. You know everyone. It'll be fun."

She points a finger at me, smiling. "I'm there."

My heart beats a little faster at that beautiful smile. I head back to my place, feeling lighter already.

~

Chloe

All I can say is thank God Brendan doesn't hold a grudge. We're hanging out again, popping into each other's apartments at all hours. I was so afraid I'd lost him forever. He's just such a good guy, and I know I can tell him anything. He really listens when I share about my work at the lab, which still isn't as great as all the interesting things I want to pursue in future research topics. He follows along surprisingly well, too, considering he never studied bio and chem past high school. He's smart, warm, and so good humored it makes me feel light and happy just being around him.

But there are moments.

Fierce moments that steal my breath, where the chemistry between us is such a powerful force I'm dying to cross the line, even as I'm terrified it'll ruin everything. How can I keep him as a friend when I feel so much more? I'm not sure how much longer I can resist him. Sara told me before that when the right person comes along, no matter how scary it feels, it's worth taking a risk. She speaks from experience, but it seems like her taking a chance on Adrian was a lot less risky. They were childhood friends with years to build trust in each other before they crossed the line. Not at all the same thing here. She also said I tend to shut down when things get too intense, but it doesn't feel that way with Brendan. I don't shut down at all. In fact, after I see him, I'm so wired, my nerves raw and exposed, it takes hours to settle enough to sleep. I'm too open to him, too vulnerable, and the crazy part is I *still* don't want to let him go. Does that mean he's the right person for me? Am I the right person for him? I just don't know.

I pace my apartment, my legs jittery with nerves, my chest tight. He'll be here soon to pick me up for the Fourth of July barbecue, and I'm afraid I've built this weekend up too much in my mind. I made a deal with myself to take the holiday weekend off for the sole purpose of spending as much time with him as possible. It's the only way to know if he's the right person to take a risk on.

He knocks on the door using our secret knock, which is rapid tapping like a woodpecker. It's just annoying enough to be funny. Except my breathing accelerates too much to laugh.

"Just a minute," I say, forcing a cheerful tone. I close my eyes and picture Sara with her warm eyes and loving smile, encouraging me to take a chance. My mind flashes to her and Adrian sitting close on the sofa, gazing at their beautiful baby. I calm thinking of sweet baby Henry.

I open the door. "Happy Fourth of July!"

His smile is warm, taking me in, and my jitters disappear. "Look at you, all red, white, and blue."

I do a small curtsy. "Thank you." I'm wearing a white tank top and blue jeans with a red cardigan tied around my waist for later. I figure we'll stay out late to watch fireworks and it might get cool. "And where's your red, white, and blue?"

He looks down at himself and pats himself over. "It's here somewhere."

I laugh. He's wearing a black T-shirt with black basketball shorts. "Are you wearing American flag boxers?"

He lifts the waistband of his shorts, peeks down, and does a double take like he's shocked at what he's wearing. "Tasmanian devil." He's so funny.

"Really?"

He inclines his head. "Wanna peek?"

My cheeks flush. "Let's go." I brush past him.

"Sure?" he teases, holding the door for me.

"Yes, I'm sure," I say over my shoulder with a laugh.

"I'll wear an American flag like a cape later," he says as we head downstairs. "Like Super American Man."

"You mean Captain America."

"General America. I like to think of myself more like a general."

"Of course you do."

He pushes the heavy front door open, holding it for me. I duck under his arm into the bright sunshine of a perfect summer day shimmering with promise.

"Chloe," a deep voice calls.

I turn and freeze, my stomach dropping. "Michael," I whisper.

He crosses to us and glares at Brendan before turning back to me. "I saw you with him in Villroy. Are you a couple now?"

My head spins. I can't believe he's here, all the way from

Villroy. How did he find me? Then I remember I gave him my address to mail back my stuff. "Michael, I had no idea you planned to visit."

He crosses his burly arms over his chest. "Obviously."

Brendan offers his hand to shake. "We haven't officially met. Brendan Rourke."

Michael ignores him.

I turn to Michael. "Brendan's my neighbor and friend. We were just on our way out to a barbecue."

"Chloe, can I talk to you alone?" Michael asks.

A horrifying thought occurs. "Wait, did something happen with Sara?"

"No, she's fine," he says. "This is just between you and me."

I relax a little and glance at Brendan. His jaw is tight, his entire body tense. "I'll just be a minute, okay?"

I gesture Michael farther away down the sidewalk. I don't want to invite him up to my place. I want to keep this public because I have a feeling this is going to go very, very badly. For him to travel so far just to see me, especially when I'll be visiting Villroy soon, well, it's not something a casual friend does.

"What is it, Michael? Why did you come here? I told you I'd be visiting Sara in a few weeks."

"I knew you'd be off work today, and I couldn't wait any longer to see you."

I worry my lower lip. "You didn't need to come all this way."

He puts a hand on my arm. "I love you. I'm never going to stop loving you, and this time apart has been so..." His voice catches. "So very hard. I realized my mistake. I wasn't giving your job the consideration it deserves, that you deserve. I shouldn't have asked you to do your medical training in France. I decided I'll move to the US to be with you."

I gasp. "No, Michael, don't do that. You have a great job in Villroy with free housing and everything. There's nothing like that for you here."

His voice is gruff with emotion. "My job means nothing compared to you."

My heart sinks because I just don't feel what he feels. I glance over my shoulder at Brendan, a surge of affection rushing through me just at the sight of him. That's when it hits me—Brendan's in my heart already, even though I thought I'd kept it firmly closed. He must be the right person for me.

Brendan takes a step forward, and I shake my head. I don't want him to come over here. I swallow hard and turn back to Michael. "I'm sorry. I just don't feel the same way. I think you should go."

He glares over my shoulder. "Because of him?"

"This has nothing to do with him. It's me."

But he doesn't seem to hear me. He strides over to Brendan and gets in his face. *Shit!* The two of them square off.

I rush over. "Back away. Brendan is a friend, Michael."

He doesn't take his eyes off Brendan, glaring at him, nearly nose to nose.

I appeal to Brendan instead. "Please, Bren, let's just go."

Brendan's eyes narrow, his voice a fierce growl. "You lay a hand on me, a Rourke, and your job is over. I'll have you banished from Villroy forever. Your duty is to protect the Rourke family no matter what."

"Don't tell me my duty," Michael snaps. But he backs up a step.

"Glad we understand each other," Brendan says.

Michael glares at him before pointing at me. "Here's something you should understand about Chloe. She's heartless. An empty shell of a person. Did she tell you she never cries? Not even when her parents died."

"Michael!" I shared that in confidence.

He goes on. "She went mute, shutting out the world." He shakes a finger at Brendan. "She'll shut you out too. That's what she does."

"You should leave," Brendan says to him quietly.

Michael takes a step toward me. "Chloe—"

Brendan grabs his arm, pulling him away from me.

Michael whirls and tosses Brendan to the sidewalk in one swift move.

I rush to Brendan, leaning over him protectively, and look over my shoulder at Michael. "Go away!"

Michael's lip curls. "You want him because he's royal? You're just like your sister, climbing above your station. You're no better than me, a penniless orphan nobody wanted."

I blink, speechless. That's what he thinks of me? I always had Sara. And she wasn't reaching above her station. She and Adrian were friends since they were kids. I told Michael that before. He's just trying to hurt me.

Brendan stands, and I join him. He wraps an arm protectively around my shoulders. "She told you to go."

I glare at Michael and speak in a low tone, fury in every syllable. "My sister is the best, most loving, most selfless person I know. I hope one day I'm just like her, and that has nothing to do with who she married. Don't ever talk about my sister like that again, or I'll be sure her husband hears about it. You'll be out on your ass so fast your head will spin."

"You're incapable of love," he snaps before stalking away.

I swallow hard, the words stinging because they have a ring of truth to them. I've always feared I couldn't truly love. I love my sister and my nephew, but that's different. Maybe I'm not capable of giving Brendan the love he deserves, which means I'm not the right person for him. No, I can't let Michael decide that for me. He's angry and lashing out. My gut churns, doubt lingering in my mind.

"You defended me," Brendan says, shifting to face me. "You put your petite little body between manly me and a trained assassin."

I check him over, suddenly worried. "He threw you to the concrete. Are you hurt anywhere? Do we need the first-aid kit?"

He tucks a lock of hair behind my ear. "You're not heartless, Chloe."

"I know." *I'm broken.* The awful truth stays with me.

He cups my cheek. "And *I* know you feel something for me."

I swallow hard, my stomach fluttering, nerves racing through me. I want to agree, but what comes out is, "We're friends."

His eyes are kind, his tone gentle. "I think it's time we stop denying what's between us."

"I'm not denying."

"Then kiss me."

My heart pounds, and my hands actually shake. I don't want him to know how much taking that step terrifies me, so I bluff my way through. "What will that prove? Are you trying to get me to hook up with you?"

"Sure. Let's hook up."

He's way too casual about what is a huge deal for us!

I'm furious and scared and shaken from Michael's unexpected visit and his harsh words. I lift my chin, closing my hands into fists to stop their trembling. "Fine. We'll hook up, and then you'll see it'll ruin everything—" my voice hitches "—and you'll be sprinting out the door."

"Wanna bet?"

We stare at each other for a tense moment.

I don't know who moves first, but we slam together, kissing wildly right there on the sidewalk. Brendan's strong arms wrap around me, the only thing keeping me anchored in the storm of feelings raging through me. All my lust, all my bottled-up emotion pour into the kiss. I'm out of control.

He breaks the kiss long moments later and hugs me tight. My entire body relaxes. I feel safe in his arms, and I'm not trembling anymore. His voice is husky, rumbling through his chest. "Upstairs."

It's not a question.

It was always going to come to this. I knew it the first time we got close.

He holds his hand out to me, and I take it, following him back into the building and upstairs.

14

———

Chloe

He unlocks the door to his apartment, grabbing my hand again and taking me to his bedroom. No pretty words, no seduction. He's straight and to the point. This is a man I understand.

He stops next to the bed and pulls me close. His big hand cradles my jaw, his gaze smoldering. "Chloe, I've waited so long for this."

I still. "Did you ever want to be my friend? Or was that just a way to get us to this moment?"

His eyes widen. He recovers himself and frames my face with his hands. "I wanted to be close to you in any way I could. I ignored the attraction, even though it was torture. I just need to be with you."

My breath catches. *He needs to be with me. Not want, need. No one's ever needed me for anything.* "Why?"

"Because you're unique. I'll never meet another woman as brilliant and sexy and fun as you ever again."

I blink, stunned. I've heard brilliant before, but I've never been called fun in my life. And only the guys I've slept with called me sexy. "You're the fun one."

"We're fun together." He dips his head to kiss me gently. "Why are you so short?"

I giggle. He's nearly a foot taller. I give his chest a playful shove, directing him to the bed. He takes the hint and sits on the bed, pulling me onto his lap, straddling him.

"Much better," he says against my lips before sealing his mouth over mine. I tilt my head, deepening the kiss, and his tongue spears inside. Desire pools low in my belly. His hand slides to my ass, keeping me close as lust floods me. The kiss turns wild, out of control, as the fire ignites between us.

He breaks the kiss and pulls my tank top over my head, tossing it behind me, and then makes short work of the bra. He caresses my breasts, cupping them as his mouth crashes over mine again. My fingers spear through his hair, sharp need building. His thumbs strum across the tight, hard points of my nipples, shooting pleasure through me. I grab the bottom of his shirt and rip it off.

He sets me on my feet and strips me out of my tied cardigan, jeans, and panties. Then he strips too, his gaze eating me up. As soon as he's naked, I launch myself at him.

He falls back on the mattress, taking me with him, and then rolls on top of me, resting his forearms on the mattress on either side of my head. He strokes my cheek. "Chloe." His voice is husky, his gaze tender.

"Bren," I whisper.

He cradles my jaw and kisses me deeply. I spread my legs further, needing more. But he's in no hurry, kissing me like he has all the time in the world. Then he shifts, kissing a trail along my jaw and down my throat.

"Why're you being so gentle?" I blurt.

He dips his tongue in the notch of my collarbones and kisses a hot trail along one collarbone. I move restlessly under him.

He lifts his head. "Because it's our first time making love."

"I like fucking better."

His lips twitch. "Love that mouth." He places a soft kiss at the corner of my mouth and then the other corner. My lips part on a sigh. He traces my mouth with a finger, studying my lips before nipping my lower lip and then sucking on it. Pleasure spears through me.

He takes my earlobe between his teeth and gives it a tug. His lips brush across my earlobe before he says, "I plan to take my time."

I moan.

He lifts himself enough to slide a hand between my legs, stroking me lazily. "Would you like it if I took you deep and hard?"

"Yesss," I hiss as his fingers work a slow, sensual spell, his voice nearly hypnotic.

"And then, on the second round, I lift you over me and make you sit on my face." His fingers thrust inside me as his thumb strums a steady rhythm.

My breath comes harder, but I still manage to say, "Yes." He shifted next to me at some point. I'm too lost in pleasure to care.

"And then I'll turn you around and impale you on me." He does something with his fingers that makes me see stars. My hips rock mindlessly, white-hot pleasure flooding me.

His voice is gravelly. "I'll let you ride me at your own rhythm until I take control, taking what I need while you beg me for release."

Everything in me coils tight, imagining what he describes at the same time as he works me with his fingers. I moan softly, the need so all-consuming, my release just out of reach.

Suddenly his touch is light as a feather. My eyes fly open. "Please, Bren."

His mouth crashes over mine, his fingers picking up the pace. My hips arch, and he pushes them back down, continuing his sensual torture.

I moan deep in my throat.

He breaks the kiss. "I love your throaty moans. Give me more of that, Chloe."

And then he shifts down my body, down, down, down, his mouth closing over my center. I grip his hair, tugging mindlessly, throaty cries ripped from my throat. His mouth is wicked, his fingers relentless, pushing me on and on. *Yes!* This is what I needed. My entire body bows, and I break, the orgasm crashing through me in a hard rush of pleasure. I collapse, panting.

He shifts, rising over me, pausing to suckle my breast in tight tugs. I moan softly. He leaves me long enough to reach for a condom in the nightstand. Then finally he's where I want him, wedging himself between my legs. I wrap my legs high around his waist, and he takes me in one hard thrust, letting out a low moan of his own.

He holds my jaw as he thrusts slow and deep. Our gazes lock, our breaths mingling, our bodies as close as two people can be. It's powerful, overwhelmingly so. Emotion clogs my throat. I close my eyes, unable to hold the intensity of the moment.

He shifts away, only he's just repositioning us, kneeling between my legs and lifting my ankle over his shoulder. He kisses my calf gently before lifting the other leg over his shoulder and kissing that calf too. Then he grabs my hips and drives into me hard, stealing my breath. My gaze catches on his as pleasure consumes me. He slides one hand in a trail from my throat to my breast, pinching the nipple hard, making me gasp before continuing a soft trail down my stomach and delving between my legs. His strokes are featherlight, his thrusts hard. All of me lights up.

His eyes gleam. He seems to know what I need before I can voice it. My body tightens around him, the pleasure ratcheting up.

"Bren," I practically beg.

His eyes lock on mine, and it's all there—the pleasure, the love, the tenderness. And then the demand. "Now," he growls.

I break, a starburst of pleasure radiating through me as he holds me tight to him, thrusting roughly, bringing more and more pleasure. His harsh moan as he lets go sends another thrill through me.

He releases his hold on me and settles behind me, maneuvering me into a spooning position. He kisses my shoulder. "Baby, as soon as I recover, I'm gonna take you just like this."

He pulls my leg back over his. "You'll be wide open for deep fucking."

I shiver. He paints an erotic picture that excites me more than I thought possible just from words. "We're going to be late for your family's barbecue."

"We'll be there in time for dinner instead of lunch."

"Won't they be wondering where you are?"

"Priorities, Chloe. This has been a long time coming." He turns my head toward him and kisses me soundly on the mouth. "You like when I'm aggressive. You need it."

"It gets me out of my head," I admit, turning back on my side and settling into his pillow. "I spend too much time in my head."

His voice is a rumble by my ear. "I need it too. We're a good match."

Nerves run through me. "Oh, Blaze." *Wrong guy, ha-ha.* I need to keep it light, ease into this.

He nips my neck. "Blaze." I can hear the smile in his voice.

The question immediately pops into my mind that I don't dare ask: *now what?*

Brendan

I watch as Chloe lifts her jaw, examining her neck in the bathroom mirror. "Do I have beard burn?"

"Nah." *Yeah.*

We've been at it for hours, but I want her again. I wrap my arms around her waist from behind and nuzzle into her exposed neck. "Just be glad I didn't give you a hickey." I suck on the cord of her neck. Not too hard. We're heading to my parents' house after this.

"Bren." She sounds breathless. "Hickeys are so high school."

"Thank you." I slide a hand under her tank top, stroking up her side. "Hey, didn't I predict you'd break your celibacy vow by the Fourth of July? And here we are."

"It wasn't a vow, so much as..." She gasps as I pinch her

nipple. "We can't be any later. They're expecting us." She pushes my hand away.

I caress her sweet ass in tight jeans instead. "What's another hour? We gotta make up for lost time." I'm feeling greedy.

She turns to face me. "We're more than two hours delayed already. By the time we get there, it'll be way past fashionably late."

"I'll just say you couldn't resist me. Everyone will understand." I slide my hand down her ass and cup her underneath. Then I caress her, back and forth between her legs. She leans weakly against me. She's hot to the touch, even through her jeans. I've got the *melt Chloe* touch.

I nuzzle her neck and let my teeth scrape against her as I stroke her.

Her fingers grip my shirt. "Bren." Her voice is breathy, urgent.

"Once more," I tell her as I undo the button on her jeans and turn her so her back is to my front. I kiss along the column of her neck before stripping her out of her jeans and panties, my fingers immediately delving between her legs.

She grips the counter for balance. "Be quick," she says over her shoulder.

I give her a devilish grin. "Baby, there is nothing gonna be quick about this." I strip down, condom on—yup, I came prepared—and then I bend her over the counter.

Her breath shudders out, but I don't hear a word of complaint about my slow pace. She's too busy moaning as I pump deep inside her while my fingers tease, feathering the lightest touch over pleasure central. It's so satisfying, feeling her usual careful control fray and then unravel entirely. She rocks her hips, already desperate for more of my touch. I work on making her crazed, alternating firm strokes and light touches, until we're both covered in a fine sheen of sweat. Me from holding back, her from raw need.

"Don't stop, don't stop," she chants.

I send her over, and she cries out, her body squeezing me rhythmically, nearly taking me with her. My own need claws at me. I grab her hips and pull her back onto me tight, stilling her. She pants under me, her head dropping.

I lift her knee to the counter, opening her fully, and thrust again. She gasps. *Oh yeah, that is good.* Slow thrusts feel like heavenly torture. She's moaning softly again, making me harder.

"I need you to come again, baby," I whisper in her ear, giving her a light tap between the legs. Her hips jerk.

I gentle my touch, and she moans long and low. It's a beautiful sound.

I stroke her lightly, my thrusts deep, pushing us both closer and closer to the edge. Her hips rock to my rhythm, right there with me, her skin fever hot under mine. I amp up the pace, unable to hold back much more. She breaks on a harsh cry, and I let go, pumping fiercely as an explosion of pleasure rockets through me. My own guttural groan mixes with her soft sounds of pleasure.

I lower her leg to the ground, but I don't release her. I hold her tight to me for a moment longer, my arms wrapped around her.

"That was definitely not quick," she says with a breathy laugh. "But I feel too good to be mad about being so late."

I let her up and turn her to face me, framing her face with my hands and kissing her. "It seemed a challenge."

Her eyes sparkle, her cheeks flushed pink. "Telling you to be quick is a challenge?"

"Damn straight. The devil in me said to see how long I could draw it out."

"Filing that one away for later."

"Why? So you can challenge me again?"

"Oh, yeah. At the risk of giving you a big head—"

"I'll never say no to you giving me head."

She smiles. "This is the best sex I've ever had. By a long shot, and I've had great sex. You just seem to know what I need when I need it."

I pinch her chin, elated with her confession. "I'm taking what I need, and it naturally matches what you need. You know what that means?"

"What?" she whispers.

"You're meant for me."

She swallows audibly and looks away. "We should go. Right?"

I let it slide. She pulls away when things get intense, just a bit, enough to let me know she's feeling something deep. For me, it's been building over the last month. I can wait for her to get comfortable with it. But not for too long. She leaves for Villroy in a little over three weeks. I need to know she's mine before she goes. Because once she gets back, she'll be in serious student mode and won't have much time for me. I need to build a solid foundation sooner rather than later.

I get myself back in order and give her some privacy to clean up and prepare for the next event—hanging with my family. They can be fun, but everyone together gets loud. She's used to a quieter pace of life.

I take a seat on the sofa to wait. A short while later, she steps out of the bathroom and blows out a breath. I close the distance, something telling me she's not as happy as when I left her post-orgasm just a short while ago.

Her gaze locks on mine for a charged moment before she looks away, smoothing her hair. That's when I realize her hand is shaking.

"You don't have to be nervous," I say. "You know everyone."

"I'm not. I'm fine." She crosses her arms, tucking her hands out of sight.

I pull her hands apart and hug her. She lets me, pressing her cheek against my chest. I rest a hand on her head, holding her to me, and don't say a word. Something's bothering her, and I don't even know what question to ask that won't get a quick denial. She keeps her cards close to her chest.

Finally, she speaks quietly, "Us crossing the line is a lot for me. I'm afraid I'm going to lose what we have, our close friendship. I'm afraid it was a big mistake."

"It was inevitable." I kiss her hair. "And I'll always be your friend."

She looks up at me, doubt mixing with hope in her expression. "I'm not great with emotional stuff. I know Michael filled you in—"

"He doesn't know what he's talking about. He was pissed and lashing out because you don't have deep feelings for him."

She looks away. "There's some truth to it."

It feels like she's warning me away, making sure I don't expect too much from her. Two can play at that game. "Yeah, well, I've never had a relationship before, so expect me to suck at it."

Her eyes search mine. "We officially have a relationship? Just because we…hooked up?"

"No, because we already did have a relationship. Now we just have a physical expression of it."

A small smile curves her sexy lips. "You sound so…"

"Awesome."

"Knowledgeable and mature—"

"How dare you call me mature." I give her my back and take a knee. "Climb on."

"You want me to climb on your back like a horse?"

I laugh. "Ride 'em, cowgirl. I know how you operate." I'm referring to sex, of course. Her in reverse cowgirl was a lot of fun in round two.

"You put me in that position."

"And you fucking loved it." I gesture her on. "Time's a-wasting."

She climbs on gingerly, like she's never had a piggyback ride. I give her a boost when I stand, making sure she's secure. She yelps at the sudden movement.

I swat her ass. "Settle down back there. We've got places to go."

She rests her chin on my shoulder and smiles widely. "And we would've been there already if you hadn't insisted on more sex."

I head for the door. "Can you blame me? It's been torture with your sexy self so close yet so far."

"Wait! My purse is on the coffee table."

I gallop back for it, and she laughs, a deep belly laugh I've never heard from her. I love that I brought that out. She deserves to have many happy laugh-out-loud moments in her life. I lean sideways, snag her small purse by the strap, and hand it to her. Then we head out the door.

"Whoa, horsie," she says when we reach the end of the hallway. "Not the stairs."

I set her down and give her a quick kiss. "Time to face the Rourkes." I head downstairs, and she keeps up.

At the bottom of the stairs, she swats my ass and hurries out the door. My serious studious girlfriend is playing with me.

I catch up with her outside. She beams, backing away, hoping I'll chase her. I fake a lunge, and she squeaks, turns tail, and runs. I hunt her down easily, wrap my arms around her, and swing her back around. She wiggles in my arms.

"Wrong direction," I say.

"Maybe I was just trying to get away from you."

I bite her earlobe and growl, "No chance."

She shivers before relaxing completely against me. Oh, yeah, this one is mine.

15

Chloe

I'm in unknown territory with Brendan, feeling too much too fast. We're almost at his parents' house, and the euphoric feeling from earlier has faded into raw terrifying vulnerability. My chest is tight, making it hard to get a deep breath. I need to get myself back under control. I mean, who's to say we even have a future? We're in two different places in our lives. He's settled into a career, and I'm just at the start of my journey, which is a long one. I don't know why I hadn't considered this major problem before. It's not as simple as figuring out if we're right for each other. Emotions have clogged all the logical pathways of my brain. I need to focus on my big plan. I have a plan, years in the making, and it didn't include him. I always saw myself alone.

He takes my hand and guides me through the front room of his parents' rowhouse, oblivious to my turmoil. "Everyone's probably out back."

It's a long space with the pocket doors separating the rooms open—living room in front, kitchen in center, and dining room in back.

"Hey, you made it," Garrett says, stepping inside and heading to the kitchen. "Dad's irritated you're so late without a word. Bad form, bro." He smiles at me. "Good to see ya,

Chloe. What're you still doing hanging around with this guy?"

Brendan jabs a finger at him and narrows his eyes in a threatening glare. "Watch it, Beast."

Garrett waves him on. "Bring it. I can so take you now. Unlike when we were kids."

Brendan stalks over to the kitchen, squaring off with him.

My eyes widen. Garrett is jacked. There's a reason they call him Beast. I don't doubt he could take on Brendan despite how fit and muscular he is too.

"Don't touch him." My voice comes out harsh.

Both men turn toward me in surprise.

"He's had enough rough stuff for today," I say, thinking of his confrontation with Michael.

Garrett smiles widely. "Cool, whatever."

My cheeks heat as I realize it sounds like I'm implying Brendan and I did some rough bondage or something.

Brendan's eyes go soft. "Chloe, baby, come here."

I'm too embarrassed to move. He walks over, pulls me into his arms and kisses me.

Garrett whistles a jaunty tune as he gets a couple of bottled waters out of the refrigerator. He winks at me. "Nice how you stand up for your man. See ya out there."

"He's not my man," I mutter. That sounds like we're married or something.

As soon as the door shuts behind him, Brendan turns to me. "I'm not your man?"

I have to be honest with him. "I'm a bad bet."

"Yeah, well, I'll take that bet all day long. Come on." He takes my hand and guides me through the dining room to the back door. "We have to make the rounds before I can get you alone again."

"Wow," I mutter. "You've got incredible sexual stamina." We already did it three times today.

He pushes the door open and holds it, waiting for me to go through. It's loud in the backyard between a speaker blasting Neil Diamond and the gathering of people talking and laughing. "Incredible what?" he asks.

I pitch my voice over the noise, "Sexual stamina." My voice rings out just as the song ends.

The crowd goes silent, all eyes on us.

"Now we know what made him so late," one of his brothers quips.

Everyone laughs.

I'm so mortified I don't know whether to turn tail and run, or insist we were delayed for nonsexual reasons. My full-body blush is a dead giveaway.

His mom speaks up in a tight voice. "Brendan, Faith is here." She gestures to a pretty brunette woman in a modest short-sleeved floral dress standing by her side.

Brendan mutters a curse under his breath. *Who's Faith?* She's in her twenties, a kind of wholesome-looking girl next door. She smiles sweetly at Brendan. *Is she an ex?*

Everyone is still staring at us standing on the deck, which is beginning to feel like a stage. He ambles down the steps, and I follow directly behind him, letting his big body hide my blushing face.

His mom joins us. "Hi, Chloe, I didn't realize you'd be here."

"Hi." I turn to Brendan in question, and he shrugs.

His mom smiles brightly. "Well, the more the merrier." She narrows her gaze on Brendan. "I've been wanting you to meet Faith. She's new in town, and I thought you might like to spend some time together." She holds her hand out to me. "Chloe, why don't you come sit with me?"

Oh my God. His mother set him up.

I don't know whether to laugh or run screaming from the yard. My nerves feel raw and exposed. I'm physically and emotionally spent in a way I've never been before. Now that we've crossed the line, being with Brendan is almost too much for me to handle.

He grabs my hand, keeping me anchored at his side. I glance over and the tips of his ears are bright red. "Mom, Chloe and I are together."

Faith stares at the ground, blushing.

I feel bad for her. Brendan did tell his mom that we were just friends at Jack's wedding.

"You coulda kept me up to date," his mom says through her teeth. "Didn't you get my text saying I wanted you to meet her?"

"Yes," Brendan replies, also through his teeth. "I just didn't know you were going to force the issue."

"I should go," Faith says.

"No," his mom says. "Please stay. You just got here." She turns to us. "How about we all sit and have some dessert?"

Faith looks at Brendan shyly.

I have no idea what to do.

"Who's up for horseshoes?" his dad calls from the far corner of the yard by the horseshoe pit.

Brendan takes off.

Grr…

His mom hustles me and Faith over to a round patio table with an umbrella for shade, where a dessert platter catches my attention. Chocolate cupcakes with miniature American flag decorations on top, chocolate-chip cookies, slices of apple pie, and brownies with red, white, and blue sprinkles. My mouth waters.

Mrs. Rourke takes a seat next to a woman who looks like she could be her sister, same shoulder-length, dark brown hair, except the other woman has bangs. Mrs. Bianchi, that's right. Ariana's mom. I met her at the wedding. Then Mrs. Rourke gestures for Faith to sit next to her.

I sit next to Ariana and the baby and give them a warm hello, trying to ignore the jab over Mrs. Rourke inviting Faith to sit next to her instead of me. It doesn't mean anything. She was probably just trying to make Faith feel more at ease.

Mrs. Rourke indicates the dessert platter. "Please take one of each. We won't judge."

I take a cupcake, cookie, and brownie. "I'll save the pie for later."

"No, thanks," Faith says. "I'm watching my figure."

"Oh, you look great, honey," Mrs. Rourke says, shaking her head. "Eat, please."

"I couldn't," Faith says. And then she actually doesn't.

Mrs. Rourke introduces Faith to everyone, finishing with, "She goes to our church, and she's a kindergarten teacher too!"

Faith smiles. "I love children."

Mrs. Rourke squeezes her arm. "Me too."

Me too. Not that it matters. I eat my dessert in silence. Mrs. Rourke seems to adore Faith, a pretty, kind-hearted kindergarten teacher. I bet Faith is ready to settle down and have a family. And she lives in the neighborhood. I can't help but think she's a better fit for Brendan than I am. She wouldn't disrupt his life at all. Obviously, Mrs. Rourke is thinking along the same lines with this setup.

Becca takes the seat on my other side and sets a bottled water in front of me. "Thought you might be thirsty." She's Connor's fiancée. I met her in Villroy at Christmas and saw her at Jack's wedding too.

"Thanks," I say, surprised about the drink since I didn't ask for it.

I catch Mrs. Rourke giving her a smile and a nod. Did she text her and ask her to fetch me a bottled water? Her phone is sitting in front of her. I was distracted by dessert and my whirling thoughts. I bite into the brownie and nearly moan. It's a rich decadent chocolate, melting in my mouth.

"This is amazing," I say.

"I made the brownies," Becca says proudly. "And the cookies."

"I'm coming over to your place," I say.

She laughs. "I love baking. Con says I'm going to make him fat." She shifts, looking over to where Dylan, Brendan, Connor, and Mr. Rourke are playing horseshoes. Brendan told me earlier that his brother Sean went back to Vancouver for his wife's movie. Jack is still on his honeymoon in Hawaii. I'm starting to get to know his family.

"Just keep bringing your goodies to family parties," Ariana says, helping herself to a cookie. "Spread the sugar around so no one person overdoes it."

"I made the pasta salad," Mrs. Bianchi says to me. "When

dinner gets going, try some. You'll love it." She turns to Faith. "You too, if you decide to eat." Her tone says she doesn't approve of women who don't eat at a barbecue. I'm starting to really like Mrs. Bianchi.

"Sure," I say. "I'm not sure how long Brendan plans on staying."

Mrs. Rourke looks around the table. "I hope everyone can stay to see the fireworks with us tonight. I didn't get to chat much at the wedding last weekend, being mother of the groom."

"And having three glasses of champagne," Mrs. Bianchi says with a cackling laugh. "She can't hold her liquor."

Mrs. Rourke sits up primly and says, "That is not an insult. I only drink on special occasions."

"I never drink," I say, swallowing a bit of brownie. "I'm underage. Plus I don't want to be out of control."

"I never drink either," Faith says, smiling serenely at me.

Is she trying to best me?

I set my water down. "Well, one time I had drinks with Brendan when we were in Villroy over Christmas." I almost add that I got a little wild, but decide it's better not to bring up my ill-fated attempt at seduction. In hindsight, why did he reject me back then? For a long time I thought he wasn't attracted to me. I crane my neck to find him again, wondering what his deal is. His back is to me, so I can't catch his eye. The man is so confusing. Back then, he acted like kissing me would be like kissing his cousin, then he rejected me, and then, when we met up for a second time here in Brooklyn, he let me think he was hooking up with other women. Why did he deliberately keep me at a distance for so long only to do a complete one-eighty with all this sex and deep emotion? Was he trying to overwhelm me? 'Cuz, guess what? It's working. It was like a sneak attack the way he got under my skin.

The women titter.

I turn back to the table. "What?"

"Nothing, sweetheart," Mrs. Rourke says.

"It's obvious you're smitten," Mrs. Bianchi points out. "Can't tear your gaze away from him for long."

My cheeks flame. I don't know where to look or what to say, so I shove the rest of the brownie in my mouth. *Could we talk about anything else?*

"Now, now," Mrs. Rourke says, waving that away and shooting her a significant look. Probably because Faith is sitting right there—Brendan's potential future mate.

Mrs. Bianchi goes on blithely, "I'm just sayin', first thing she talked about was his sexual stamina. That's how they hook ya. The good ones, anyway. So, Chloe, is Brendan treating you well?"

I nearly choke on the brownie. I'm not sure if she means in or out of the bedroom, but there's only one right answer. "Yes." It's true, anyway.

I turn to look at him. He's talking to his dad, but suddenly makes eye contact, giving me a warm smile. My stomach flutters, my pulse thrumming through my veins. I give him a little wave and turn back to the table.

Every woman is smiling at me. Except Faith.

"He's smitten too," Mrs. Bianchi says with a nod. "I know the signs."

I don't know what to say to that. But I think it's true. I'm not sure how it got to this point between us. I stare at the table, lost in a swirl of confusing emotions.

Two large hands land on my shoulders and squeeze. I know those hands. I look up just as Brendan leans over me and smiles. "Hello, how's it going over here?"

I relax, having him near again. "Good."

"We're going to go soon," he says.

I'm ridiculously relieved and try not to show it.

"You just got here," Mrs. Rourke says tightly. "And you were late."

"I told ya, he's smitten," Mrs. Bianchi carols.

Faith stands, slipping her purse strap over her shoulder. "I'm going to go too. Thank you for having me."

"Oh, Faith, I'm sorry," Mrs. Rourke says, standing and putting a hand on her arm. "I'll walk you out." They head back through the house together.

We stay a few more minutes, waiting for his mom to

return to tell her goodbye. When she does, she's frowning. She pins Brendan with a stern mom look. "That was extremely embarrassing, Bren. Next time, keep me in the loop."

"Next time, don't butt into my love life," he replies calmly.

"Faith is a lovely young woman," she fires back. She glances at me. "You're lovely too, Chloe. I was just caught by surprise." She takes us both in. "I didn't know things had changed between you two."

"It's kinda new," I say quietly.

Brendan hugs his mom, kisses her cheek, and says something to her that has her smiling and patting him on the shoulder.

I lift my hand in a wave and say bye to everyone. Brendan guides me back through the house, his hand on the small of my back. We're both quiet.

I wait until we're on the sidewalk to speak. "Faith seems nice."

"I'm so sorry you got caught up in that. I had no idea."

"Why didn't you tell your mom I was coming?" I hate that I care. I'm overwhelmed by all I'm feeling, and I fear he's nowhere near where I'm at.

He lifts one shoulder. "Didn't think it mattered."

"Oh." *Ouch.*

He turns to me. "Not that you don't matter. It just didn't occur to me to mention I was bringing a guest. There's always tons of people coming in and out."

I take a deep breath. "I think Faith would be a good match for you."

He halts. "What did my mom say?"

I nod miserably. "It's true. Your mom likes her a lot. She probably saw what I saw—a kindergarten teacher who loves kids, close to your age, living in the neighborhood. It's perfect. I'm sure Faith's ready to settle down and have a family, and wouldn't you make a great dad?" My voice cracks. I'm not ready for any of that, not for a long while, and I'm holding him back.

"Chloe."

I stare at his shoulder, unable to meet his eyes. "Maybe I'm not the one for you. We're in two different places in our lives. You deserve to see who else is out there. Someone like Faith would be better suited." My chest aches, my throat unbearably tight.

"Are you done convincing me you're a bad bet?"

I nod, unable to speak over the lump in my throat.

He cradles my jaw. "First of all, you can put Faith out of your mind because I am *never* gonna be with her. That was never on the table, even before you and I got together. And second." He kisses me, tenderly this time, and it's exactly what I need, soothing my raw nerves. "I'm not going anywhere, so stop telling me you're a bad bet."

All of my worries rush to the surface because I just can't quite believe he's going to stick. No one ever does. "How come you rejected my kiss back in Villroy? Why did you let me think you were hooking up with random women? I don't understand why you acted like you didn't want me for so long." *And then blindsided me with a relationship that makes me feel so much it scares me.*

He blows out a breath. "I was trying to resist you, a losing battle. At first, I was put off by the family connection, since I'm not known for lasting relationships. I didn't want to be the cause of family tension." He tips my chin up, his eyes full of warmth and good humor. "Didn't help that your psycho ex threatened to kill me if I touched you."

"He was just peeved. He wouldn't really hurt you."

He rocks his head side to side. "Not sure I agree with you there. But, besides all that, I didn't want to be a distraction for you. You're headed for greatness, and I didn't want to get in your way. And then I finally realized I was already so into you there was no walking away."

My throat clogs with emotion. His eyes are intent on mine, like he's expecting me to say something. "Okay." It's all I can manage.

"Good," he says against my lips. Then he kisses me, leaving me in a puddle of need. My knees are weak, all of me melting.

He breaks the kiss, entwines his fingers with mine, and resumes our walk. I follow along in a daze.

I'm in love with this man. Me, the woman who never felt love beyond that of my sister. I didn't know if I was even capable of loving someone. I've felt defective for so long, not feeling as deeply as others seem to. Yet here it is, a miracle.

I think about what he said about staying out of my way and letting me do my thing. Now that we're together, how would it work?

Would he expect me to change all my plans and stay in New York? I'm not even sure if that's a possibility. I have no idea where I'll get into med school.

Would he be willing to support my dream no matter the cost to him?

I can't ask him to leave his family for me. He'd lose something wonderful. They depend on him for work too. They're a part of him. I'm the one who doesn't belong in this equation.

I've never wanted to belong so badly in my life. But will I have to give up my dream? Or him?

16

———

Chloe

I didn't know what to do about Brendan and our uncertain future, so I did absolutely nothing. The past three weeks I just enjoyed our time together. It wasn't hard to do. We're together every night, either at his place or mine, and all weekend long. He doesn't even mind giving me quiet time to study. I take more breaks than I ever have before, but I do like to keep up on the latest medical journals and read ahead for the curriculum. Last weekend Garrett finished house-sitting for Sean and Josie and moved back in with Brendan. That was okay too. Garrett's a great guy, and I feel comfortable with him. Brendan just shifted to my place for privacy when we needed it. Everything felt light and easy until today, my second to last day here. Every time I thought, *I only have one day left*, my stomach rolled, leaving a sour taste in my mouth. Brendan says he can't get off work to visit me in Villroy, which means this is it. The beginning of the end.

Now it's three a.m. and I can't sleep with all the dread building over tomorrow, my last day. I prop up on my elbows and look over at Brendan sound asleep in my bed, and sigh. I've been tossing and turning for hours. Giving up, I tiptoe out to the living room and tuck myself into the corner of the sofa with a throw blanket, staring at nothing.

I always knew I'd have to make sacrifices to do what I feel like I was born to do. But I can't let my choices hurt anyone else. I screwed things up with Michael, and I refuse to repeat history. Brendan deserves happiness with a woman who can give him things I can't, like a settled life with marriage and kids, the whole deal. That's not me, at least not for a long time. I've got too much to do in the meantime. He says he doesn't want to get in my way, but the fact is, I'm the one holding him back. He's older than me and he'll want that stuff sooner rather than later.

And I can't ask him to join me on my journey, knowing it could take me far from here. He has no idea how special his close family is because he's never experienced anything different. Never been lonely or felt broken inside by loss. I don't want that for him. He belongs here.

Brendan's warm smile flashes through my mind, making my eyes sting and my chest tighten. I clutch the blanket closer around me like a hug. I love him. I never thought I could feel so deeply for another person. For so long I was at peace, bringing all of my passion and focus to this one thing, my dream career, the thing I was put on this earth to do. Now I'm torn. I can't give up everything I've worked so hard for. But it's not fair to ask him to sacrifice his career and leave his family for me.

For the first time in my life, my head and my heart are at cross purposes. My head says to let him go, and my heart says to hang on tight no matter the cost. But he's the one who has to pay the price. I can't ask that of him. It's selfish, and that's not what love should be.

I slide down on the sofa, curling on my side, lost in a dark place of churning emotions and conflicting thoughts. Every- thing I've ever wanted is in reach. Everything I never knew I needed is there too, with him. Give up my dream or give up him? The question circles round and round in an endless painful loop in my mind.

Finally, with the first rays of the sunrise, I toss the blanket back and stand, my limbs heavy. I know what I need to do. My throat tightens painfully, and I cross my arms, hugging myself. It's the only thing I can do for his ultimate happiness—

I have to let him go.

~

I dragged through the last day of my internship, drinking multiple cups of coffee to stay awake. After that, Brendan took me to a fancy restaurant for dinner to celebrate my last day, and now we're back at my place. I loved the restaurant, a white-tablecloth, too-much-silverware kind of place. I love him. I haven't told him because I know it'll only make it harder to say goodbye. My gut churns, threatening to bring up dinner. I need a moment before I can face what needs to be done.

I hand him the TV remote. "I'm going to pack."

"Sure," he says, unbuttoning the top two buttons of his dress shirt. He looks so handsome in a light blue shirt, navy trousers, and dress shoes. He left work early to shower and change into dressy clothes for our special night.

I smile, but it's a little wobbly, my throat tight. I go to my bedroom and pull the suitcase from the closet. I have less than twenty-four hours left with Brendan. I tell myself all good things must come to an end. At least that's been my experience. It was a stroke of luck I got to be his neighbor for the summer, and I'm grateful for that. I have to hold onto those bittersweet memories.

I toss clothes into my suitcase, barely seeing them. The thing is, it's so much more than just sex with him. He makes me feel good, relaxed and secure. Like I have a stable foundation. How weird is that? Sara has always been my stable foundation, and then I made my own, which sometimes feels shaky, but I get through. He's become important to me, and it kills me that we're going to be ripped apart. I still, swallowing hard, my exhausted brain trying to focus on why this is the best course of action. His happiness, that's right. I can't give him what he deserves. All I'll do is take him away from everything good in his life.

I press my casual clothes flat to make room for my work clothes on top. I knew he'd be ripped away from me. It was inevitable. It doesn't matter that I'm the one leaving this time, the result is the same. My vision blurs for a moment, and I blink rapidly to clear it. I desperately need sleep, but first I need to…I can't be selfish. I have to draw on every ounce of strength within me to do the right thing.

After I finish packing, I change out of my work clothes and into my summer pajamas, an old T-shirt and sweatpants. Then I have second thoughts. Is this how I want Brendan to remember me on our last night together? I change again into a green tank top and jeans, my usual casual uniform.

I take a deep breath and head back to the living room, taking a seat next to him. He's watching some kind of car show, where the mechanics are fixing up a classic car. I sit quietly, trying to work up the nerve to say what I know has to be said. Something like, it's been wonderful, but we're in two different places in our lives, and I think it's best if we say goodbye now. But let's meet up again in five years if we're both still single. I know that last part is selfish, leaving a small window open for getting back together, but at least I'm giving him a chance to meet someone else. He's older than me, and I honestly don't expect him to wait around, hoping for someday. It just makes me feel better to think there's a small ray of hope.

No, I need to cut ties for his sake. He gets his freedom. Period. I wish I could just enjoy tonight. Ah, hell. He'll ultimately leave me anyway. He'll get tired of waiting around for the tiny slivers of free time in my life.

He gives me side-eye. "You seem tense."

I cross my arms and uncross them, trying to appear relaxed. "Nope."

He presses pause on his show and sets the remote down. "Do I need to take you in there—" he jerks his chin toward the bedroom "—and turn you into a limp noodle?"

I laugh a little, flushing with heat despite my inner turmoil. That's what I always say he turns me into. He just wrings me out and leaves me boneless, utterly spent. His stamina is incredible. And he's demanding, wanting everything I can give, and then wanting more. If only everything was as simple as what we have in the bedroom.

He pushes a lock of hair behind my ear. "What's wrong?"

I swallow hard. "We need to talk."

He turns off the TV. "I know. It's your last night here. I'm going to miss you, but we'll keep in touch, and I'll see you when you get back."

I bite my lower lip. "Bren, I think we should stop right here, end it on a high note."

He stares at me, his jaw gaping.

Shit. I didn't think this was going to be that big a surprise. It seemed inevitable.

I rush on. "This summer has been great, but after I get back from Villroy, I'll be working round the clock between my studies and my work at the hospital. Not to mention wrapping up my med school applications. And then I don't know where I'll be for med school. I could be thousands of miles away. Everything is so uncertain in my life, and you deserve better than that."

He works his jaw, glaring at me.

My voice comes out small. "I tried to tell you I was a bad bet."

"So you're breaking up with me?"

"It's a natural parting time."

More glaring.

I swallow over the lump in my throat. "Bren, you've somehow become my best friend. Friends can pick up whenever, no hard feelings. It's not the same with a relationship. I won't have the time or energy to devote to one. Not the way you deserve." My voice catches. "I can't give you what you deserve."

"Do I get a say in this?"

"I'm sorry." I wring my hands together and stare at them. "I don't regret our time. I'm so…thankful for what we had."

"Thankful? Thankful!" he barks, startling me.

He looks to the ceiling, takes a deep breath, and levels his gaze on me. "Chloe, I know you. You pull away when things get intense. I know we're in deep, both of us. I'm asking you to stick with me, and I swear I'll stick with you too."

"I've given it a lot of thought. It's the right thing." I swallow over the lump in my throat. "What if we stick together as best friends?" A small ray of hope shines through at the thought. I won't have to completely lose him.

"No."

My stomach drops. "No?"

"No, Chloe," he bites out. "I don't want you as a friend."

"Don't you see it's for your own good? I'm giving you your freedom."

His lips form a flat line. "For someone so smart, you're doing something really stupid." He stands and stalks to the front door.

I leap off the sofa. "You'll see I'm right. Give it time."

He stills for a moment, shakes his head, and walks out the door.

I slap a hand over my mouth, my eyes hot, my gut churning horrifically. It's over, and now he hates me. Oh God, I'm going to be sick.

I race to the bathroom and vomit. Isn't that just the perfect metaphor for the way my relationships end? Down the toilet.

17

Chloe

The next morning I walk across the tarmac to the royal jet like a zombie. I barely slept last night. I kept replaying my night with Brendan. Our dinner together, his blue eyes warm on mine, the way his deep voice seemed to reach out and caress me. And then later, my attempt to painlessly get out of his way. I hurt him, and that's what hurts me the most. But what was the alternative? Let it drag on as we gradually drift apart until there's nothing left between us? It had to end at some point. It will only hurt more postponing the inevitable.

A flight attendant meets me halfway, taking my luggage for me. "Good morning, Miss Chloe."

"Morning," I say absently. I check his name tag since I don't recognize him from previous flights. "Nice to meet you, Henry." That's my nephew's name too. At least I'll have baby Henry to comfort me.

I trudge up the stairs to the jet's entrance, my backpack over my shoulder. I plan to work on med school applications on the flight, figuring keeping my mind focused on my future goal will help manage my current agony. My eyes sting with unshed tears. I still can't seem to cry, even as horrible as I feel. I can't believe how close I got to Brendan, more than anyone in my life besides my sister, and now it's over, exactly as I always knew it would be. I just didn't anticipate this deep level of pain. Like a part of me is missing.

The jet is empty besides the pilot and copilot, who greet me warmly. I can't manage a smile, but force some energy into my voice to return the greeting.

I take a window seat in the front row and stare at the open field next to the private airport in New Jersey. *Goodbye, goodbye, goodbye.* I lean my head back on the headrest and close my eyes.

"Hello," a familiar deep voice says, landing in the seat next to me.

My eyes fly open. "Brendan! What're you doing here?"

"What does it look like I'm doing here?"

I stare at him. "Going to Villroy?"

He puts his seatbelt on. "Yup. I'll be there for a week. Put your seatbelt on."

I comply, my mind whirling. *What does this mean?*

The flight attendant checks in with us and lets us know we'll be leaving shortly.

I can't seem to put the pieces together after the way we left things last night. I thought he hated me. It doesn't help that I'm sleep deprived. "Bren, why're you going to Villroy?"

He stretches his jean-clad legs out and crosses them at the ankles. "I'm a prince. The palace is my natural habitat."

"Natural habitat," I echo.

"Mmm-hmm."

I face front, blinking a few times. Finally, I ask, "Are we friends again?"

He gives me a sideways look. "We'll talk once we've reached our cruising altitude. I want to be sure you're not going anywhere."

I gulp. Why does he think I'm going to flee the scene? What's he going to say to me that would make me want to flee? Doesn't he know I'm barely hanging on by a thread here?

"You look tired," he says.

"I didn't sleep much last night. Or the night before."

"Rest your eyes a bit."

I stare at him. "I don't think that's possible. I'm in too much shock."

He leans his head back and closes his eyes. "Shock and awe. Yup. I have that effect on people."

My brain hurts, trying to figure out what he's up to, and then the jet starts taxiing down the runway, the white noise making me drowsy.

I wake with the chime that indicates we can take our seatbelt off. I take mine off and shift to face Brendan, feeling more alert with my catnap. "Okay, talk. What's going on? Why are you here? What do you plan to do in Villroy for a week? Are we friends or not?"

"I'm here because I decided we'll keep being best friends like you wanted." He tucks a lock of hair behind my ear, drawing close, his breath hot over my lips. "I'll be your best friend and your lover." He kisses me and draws back, his eyes intent on mine.

My lips part, enthralled for a moment, and then I scowl. "That is not a thing! Best friend and a lover. You can't be both."

"Chloe, it's called a husband."

My jaw drops, my heart racing. My mind flashes back to Michael proposing just last year, but this time's different. Instead of everything in me retreating at the thought, I long to be able to say yes. But I can't. He'll be miserable tied to me. I won't be able to give him what he deserves. He'll lose too much.

My throat clogs with emotion. "You don't mean that. Take it back."

He eyes me. "This right here—" he gestures between us "—this is love. I feel it, and I know you do too. It might not be perfect timing, but…" He shrugs. "It's the real deal."

My world is tilting under me. "Suddenly you're the relationship expert."

He leans close. "It's been building all summer. Why am I your best friend?"

I take in his warm eyes, his handsome face, always ready for a smile, his solid strength. "Because I can't wait to tell you everything that happened in my day and share everything I'm planning and dreaming for the future. And I love to hear everything going on with you too."

He smooths my hair back and cradles my jaw. "And I like hearing it and telling you stuff. I look forward to dinner with you and talking and just watching TV together, yelling at the screen. We're very compatible."

"I thought we were opposites." He's the fun one. I'm not.

One corner of his mouth tilts up. "Maybe you have a little devil in you, and I have a little serious student in me."

"What are you a student of?"

He kisses me. "You. Every little fact I file away, every expression, every emotion you express. I eat it up. You've become my favorite person in the world."

A surge of affection rushes through me, my chest warming. That means a lot because he has so many awesome people in his life. "You're my favorite person too."

"Thanks."

"It's not tough competition, though. I only have my sister, my roommate, and my study group."

He pulls me into his lap, wrapping his arms around me. I know I should move away, but it feels so good to be back in his arms. Besides, where would I go? We're on a jet thousands of miles in the air. Smart man, waiting for us to be flying. Now I have to stay here, tucked close.

He shifts to meet my eyes, his voice low. "This summer with you was the longest I've ever been with a woman before we had sex. We've built something here, beyond the physical. You understand? This love isn't going anywhere."

My breath catches, a tiny bubble of hope rising in me. Still, it won't be easy. "I need you to understand what you're getting with me. I need to focus on my studies. I need to be a medical researcher. It's all I've ever wanted, to give back in a significant way."

"You will be. I want that for you."

I worry my lower lip, almost afraid to say the next part. "And if I go away for med school? My dream is Harvard."

He studies me for a long moment before squeezing me tight. "Then I'll go with you."

I push out of his arms and sit back in my seat. "What?"

"I'll go with you," he says loud and clear. I still can't believe my ears.

"And do what?"

"I'll look for a new job."

My mind whirls. "You can't abandon your family for me!"

"It's not abandoning. It's following my heart. You're my heart, Chloe."

I hold up a palm, refusing to be the reason he loses everything. "That doesn't make sense."

He places his palm against mine.

My voice chokes, my eyes hot. "You're not making sense." And then tears leak out, running down my cheeks. I'm crying. I never cry. I wipe the tears away, irritated by them.

His arm wraps around my shoulders, hauling me against his side. "Tell me why you're crying. You, the woman who never cries."

The tears just keep coming, spilling down my cheeks. I'm angry and confused and out of control. "I can't trust love! It's a cocktail of chemicals that fades in time."

He wipes my tears away with his thumbs. "That made you cry? Because you're afraid to love?"

I sniffle. "I didn't say I was afraid." *Am I?* "I said I don't trust it."

He signals to the flight attendant, Henry, who rushes over with a tissue box. It occurs to me they were expecting Brendan, and maybe he told them why. As fast as Henry arrived, he disappears toward the back of the jet, shutting a curtain behind him.

I clutch the tissue box, tears still flowing, my grasp on reality slipping. Nothing makes sense. I'm sitting on a private jet, having a private conversation with a discreet witness nearby, and the man I thought I'd never see again is promising to never leave.

Brendan grabs a tissue, hands it to me, and takes the box

from my hands. I blow my nose and try to stop the water-works. It's impossible now that the dam has broken.

"Chloe."

I peer at him through watery eyes. "What?"

"Here's how it's going to go. Part one of the plan, after Villroy, you're going back to school. We'll get together on weekends."

"What if I need to study?" My voice is wobbly.

He gives me a gentle smile, causing a fresh bout of tears to spill out of my stinging eyes. "Then I'll meet you after you're done studying, or maybe I'll help you study by quizzing you. You'll graduate, and I'll be there cheering you on. Good so far?"

I nod and gesture for another tissue. He gets it for me.

He continues. "Part two, you're going to medical school. I'll be there too. Part three, you'll become a researcher and find a cure for cancer. And somewhere between part one and part three, you'll marry me."

I stare at him blankly, blinking the tears away, trying to focus on his face. He's absolutely sincere. I never would've guessed he'd be willing to meet me more than halfway like this. It's too good to be true.

"But your family—" I start.

"Will understand." One corner of his mouth tilts up, revealing the dimple I know and love. I stroke it lightly through his beard, and he covers my hand with his, giving it a squeeze. "My dad gave up a kingdom for love, remember?"

I nod, trying to understand how this could work, so he doesn't ultimately resent what he's giving up. It's not some-thing I'd ever ask of him, but he's offered and I don't doubt his sincerity for a minute.

"Bren, that's an awfully long plan. Are you sure you want to wait around for me?"

He strokes my cheek, his gaze tender. "If I married you today, I'd be with you for life. If I marry you after medical school, I'm still with you for life. I'm not going anywhere, Chloe. You're stuck with me."

I choke on a sob and finally admit my greatest fear.

"Everyone close to me has been ripped away. What if you die?"

"Then I'll haunt you."

I scowl. "That's not possible. Ghosts aren't real."

"I'll love you in life and death." He takes my hand and places it over his heart. "Our love will live on in our hearts."

"But it didn't with my parents. I barely remember them. Sara says they loved us very much, but it's not in my heart." He wipes more tears from my face. "I've got a hole in my heart that can never be filled."

"Sara loves you very much. She gave you their love too. She carried on what your parents gave her and passed it to you. There's no hole in your heart, baby. You love me, right?"

I let out a shaky breath. "I do. I've been afraid to say it."

"Say it now."

"I love you." A calm settles over me. Lightning didn't strike me down for daring to love. The plane didn't suddenly fall from the sky. I've been afraid to truly love in case it was taken from me.

He dips his head, his voice silky by my ear. "I love you too." He gazes down at me with love in his eyes. I knew all along it was there but was afraid to trust. Now I soak it in, reveling in it.

"Bren, I love you, okay? But I had a plan. You were not in that plan."

His eyes gleam devilishly, his head tilting to the side. "I threw a wrench in the works."

"Yes!"

"Sometimes you need a wrench. It's a very useful tool." He leers at me, pulling me close for a kiss. "I can see to your plumbing."

I put a hand on his chest. "Be serious."

"I am." He kisses me again, roughly this time, distracting me as he pulls me back into his lap. The moment his arms wrap around me, my entire body relaxes. This is right. I can't deny it, and I'm starting to believe he really is in it for the long haul.

I sigh as he shifts to nuzzle into my neck. "Did I just agree to marry you?"

He lifts his head and grins. "I believe you did."

I wrap my arms around his neck and kiss him passionately. The fire ignites between us, soothing my fears like nothing else, this connection. He's mine for keeps.

A long while later, he lifts his head, his eyes heated. "Too bad there's not a bedroom on the jet."

I smile. "You can wait until Villroy."

He brushes his thumb across my lower lip. "Torture." His voice is gravelly, scraping against my insides.

I let out a shaky sigh and snuggle into his chest. I lift my head as a thought occurs. "What if things didn't work out between us? You would've been stuck with me on the jet and in Villroy."

He gives me a cocky grin. "It would've made for an awkward visit, eh? But I knew you'd succumb to my devilish charm."

I gaze into his eyes, lost in how much I feel for him. He's confident enough for both of us, and I'm starting to trust in that confidence.

He nips my lower lip and then sucks it. "You're mine."

I run my fingers through his soft hair, smiling. "Wait. You're not going to confront Michael in Villroy, are you?"

"I don't need to. It's obvious you're nuts about me."

"So cocky."

He grins. "So right."

"Are we really getting married?"

He gets serious. "I want you to graduate Columbia first. All your focus on that with no wedding distractions. Sound good?"

My eyes sting, and I press my lips together tightly, trying desperately not to cry again. "Yes. I love you so much."

He hugs me, kissing my hair. "I always knew you did."

18

———————

Ten months later...

Brendan

My heart feels like it's going to burst out of my chest. Literally. I'm so damn proud of my woman. I leap from my seat and clap as Chloe walks across the stage to accept her diploma. She graduated summa cum laude—which only the top five percent of students achieve—with a double major in biology and chemistry. After she shakes the line of deans' hands, she smiles and waves at us in the audience.

Sara's filming it with her phone like a proud mom. She practically raised Chloe, and I love her for that. My cousin Adrian's holding little Henry and whistling for Chloe, two fingers in his mouth. He's got to hold Henry now that he's twenty months old; otherwise, that kid is on the move. Chloe's roommate for the last three years, Lindsey, is sitting with us too. She's been a good friend to Chloe. They're pretty close, considering how much time Chloe spends studying. Lindsey says it's going to be tough for her to go back to school in the fall without her roomie. She doesn't graduate until next May.

I watch as Chloe takes her seat again in the mass of light

blue caps and gowns. A huge smile spreads across my face, my eyes stinging. I swear she's a genius, though she insists she's just a hard worker. How many people could do what she did? Graduate with highest honors in a double major in only three years from a top-notch university. It's remarkable, *she's* remarkable. I hope our kids take after her. That's a while away, though. She's got time. She's twenty-one now with a new challenge ahead of her—Harvard Medical School. That's right. She got in. I nearly cried with her when she got the news. All right, I did. A little. Emotions are so contagious.

I exchange a watery smile with Sara. "Our girl's a freaking genius," I whisper to her.

Sara beams. "I know! I'm so proud of her."

The rest of the ceremony drags on. I'm anxious to get to Chloe to congratulate her. This school year hasn't been too bad as far as seeing each other. We worked it out where I pick her up on Saturday night after she's finished studying and take her back to my place to spend the night. We spend all day Sunday together. That's her day off. A few times she studied a bit when she needed to, but I understood. I don't mind as long as we're together. Beast was nice enough to clear out to give us alone time on the weekends. He usually stays with Sean and Josie, who have a guest room.

I'm moving up to Massachusetts with her. It's a sweet deal since we can stay in affordable med school student housing. We'll have an apartment not far from campus. As for my job, well, it was tough to break the news to my brothers that I'd be leaving. I'm the only one who's ever fully stepped away. Dylan left the door open for me to come back if Chloe and I end up settling in New York. For the near future, I'm starting my own contracting business flipping houses. I'm psyched because I've always wanted to be my own boss and it's a job I can literally do anywhere. There's always some run-down house in need of renovation. And I know how to spot a good investment thanks to the time I've spent scouting out properties for Rourke Management.

And guess who's taking over scouting properties for me at

my old job? It's two people, actually, my dad and my sister-in-law Ariana. It's a great fit for them since my dad has his real estate license and Ariana used to work for a real estate development company. She works from home, so she can have a flexible schedule with the baby. So I feel good about that too. My work continues to be in the family's hands.

Finally, Chloe rejoins us. She beams. "I did it!"

Sara gets to her first, hugging her and crying. "You did! My brainiac sister. I'm so proud of you!" Chloe hugs her back, smiling at me over her sister's shoulder.

The moment Sara lets her go, I pull Chloe into my arms. "Congratulations, graduate. I'm so proud of you too." I frame her face with my hands and kiss her. "I'm in awe."

She cups my jaw, stroking my beard. "Thank you, Bren. And thank you for being so patient with me this year."

"Worth it."

Adrian and Lindsey congratulate her next, and Chloe kisses Henry's chubby cheek, exclaiming over how big he's gotten.

We join the crowd filing out. Adrian arranged for a limo to take us to a fancy Italian restaurant for a celebratory lunch. The place was my choice because they have great tortellini and I want to remind Chloe of our first "date," making tortellini together while trying to resist each other. I always knew that was a losing battle. Ha. So worth the month of torture just to get to know her better. She got into my heart. I have something special planned for Chloe at the restaurant too.

～

Chloe

We're at a round table for six in a classy Italian restaurant for my graduation-day lunch. It's me, Brendan, Sara, Adrian, Lindsey, and Henry in a high chair. I'm between Brendan and Henry. I have to soak in my nephew while I can. I love the little guy.

"I'm so glad to be out of my cap and gown," I say. "It was getting hot under there."

"You looked amazing," Sara says. "Like a scholar."

I smile. It's a pretty great feeling to graduate after three years of hard work. I know I have four years of med school ahead of me, which isn't easy by any stretch of the imagination, but I have a break between now and then. Move-in day for med school is August second. This summer I'm devoting to enjoying myself with my best friend and lover, the phenomenal Brendan Rourke. Brendan and I sort of learned together how to navigate our relationship. We're each other's first love, which I think is pretty special.

He lifts my chin. "You're gazing at me worshipfully again. Keep it up." He kisses me and grins.

I'm so crazy about him and let him know so often he's gotten a big head about it. "Always the modest one."

"Someone has to be, Ms. Summa Cum Laude. I swear I'm calling Mensa to have you tested."

I shake my head, smiling. "Stop. You know I work my ass off. It's dedication to your chosen interest that makes the results look easy. If I really was a genius, I wouldn't have sweated my way through finals." I actually do sweat. My brain is working so hard I sweat through exams like a workout.

The waiter appears to read us the specials. And one of them is freshly made tortellini!

I turn to Brendan. "Tortellini! I'm definitely getting that. Remember when we made it? It was so hard, but fun too."

He grins and takes in the table. "Chloe and I were pseudo-friends for a month last summer and made tortellini together."

Everyone smiles at us.

I cock my head. "Wait, pseudo-friends? No, we were actual friends."

He gives me a deadpan look. "Do not pretend you weren't fighting major chemistry the whole time."

"Busted!" Lindsey crows. Her hair is short and back to its natural brown. I kinda miss the purple she had before. "I heard all about the hot neighbor living next door that she had to keep in the friend zone."

"Lindsey!" I exclaim. "Those desperate texts were private."

We laugh.

A short while later, I'm enjoying tortellini. So is Brendan. "What do you think?" I ask him. "Better than ours?" I'm teasing. This is way better.

"Considering it was our first time cooking a real dinner, I'd say…" He laughs. "Theirs is way better. I think we cooked ours too long, it was kinda chewy. And some of them hardly had any meat filling. But I did love it because we made it together."

My heart squeezes. I want to kiss him, but I don't want to get all mushy in front of my sister's family and Lindsey. Instead I just smile and turn to Henry, offering him one of my tortellini. He has a tiny bowl of mac 'n cheese that he's mostly been ignoring. He chews the tortellini eagerly and grunts, leaning forward and doing the sign for more. Sara taught him baby signs since he's a late talker. All he says is mama, dada, and no.

After we finish eating and the dishes are cleared, Brendan says to me, "I got you a cake."

"You did?" I rub my full stomach. "You should've told me so I'd save room."

"There's always room for cake."

I shake my head. "I don't know. I might just have a bite of yours."

Sara catches me up on the latest with the casino she runs with Adrian, which is always a fascinating update. They do a lot of cool stuff as far as events and new games to attract repeat customers.

Brendan whispers in my ear, "Look."

I turn just as a waiter sets down a round chocolate cake with a giant sparkler on top of it. Gold sparks fizzle out of the skinny stick. I've never seen a celebration cake like that before. Usually it's just boring candles.

"How cool!" I turn to Henry, whose eyes are wide as

saucers, his mouth hanging open. He thinks it's cool too. I take in the rest of the table for their reaction. They're all smiling at me. I smile back. Lindsey lifts her brows, pointing over to Brendan.

I turn, but he's not there. And then I realize his chair has been pushed out of the way because he's down on one knee, holding up a diamond ring to me.

My hand flies to my mouth, my eyes watering. He said he wanted me to graduate before we were engaged. I just didn't know he meant the same day.

"Chloe, you are my world, my heart, my forever love. My first, my last. Will you be my wife?"

I nod, unable to speak over the lump in my throat. He slides the ring on my finger and stands, pulling me into his arms. I wrap my arms around his waist and squeeze him tight, my tears soaking his nice shirt.

He strokes my hair. "I love you."

I lift my head. "I love you too!"

"Yay!" Sara exclaims. "Congratulations! I was prepared and got a bunch of pictures of the proposal. C'mere, let me see this rock."

I laugh and walk over to her, showing off a simple round solitaire on a gold band. It's perfect. "So you all knew he was going to propose?"

She smiles and nods. Adrian and Lindsey smile too.

"I was so excited," Lindsey says. "It was so hard to keep it a secret."

I turn to look at Brendan, who's seated now while the waiter returns to slice the cake. Brendan smiles at me tenderly, his eyes soft. "I wanted your family to be here for it." He turns to Lindsey. "You're an honorary sister, so you're in."

Lindsey beams at me. I give her a watery smile, suddenly realizing just how lucky I was to have such a wonderful roommate these last three years. She always made time to have fun with me, even though she had a group of other friends she went out with too. I go over and hug her. "I'm going to miss you."

"I'll miss you too," she cries, throwing her arms around me. "School won't be the same without my roomie."

I sniffle and wipe more tears. "I'll stay in touch. I'm sure you'll have a great senior year." We talk for a few more minutes and then I take my seat.

Brendan feeds me a bite of his cake.

"Mmm, it's so good! I just wish I had room for it."

"I'll get a slice to go for you," he says. "Got you covered."

I smile at him with all the love in my heart and then take in my family, my heart full to bursting. "This is the happiest day of my life," I manage over the lump in my throat.

Sara raises her glass to me. "To many more!"

For the first time I look to the future not just as a long haul of work, but as a bright shiny adventure full of great times to come. It's love that's opened my heart to more possibilities. It's Brendan, the love of my life.

"Hear, hear," Adrian says, lifting his glass and clinking it to Sara's. Then we all clink glasses around the table.

I let out a happy sigh. Graduating after all my hard work and getting engaged to the love of my life—best day ever.

Brendan

I back Chloe up against the wall the moment I get her alone at my place. It's the middle of the week, so Beast is at work. "Finally, I get you all to myself." I kiss her and then boost her up so she can wrap her legs around me. She clings to my shoulders as I deepen the kiss.

She breaks the kiss, looking way too serious. "As much as I love getting naked with you, I have a question."

I still, suddenly wary. "What?"

"I'm happy to be your wife whenever, but would you mind if we wait on kids until I finish my residency?"

I'm so relieved it's nothing bad, a surge of energy goes through me. It's pure happiness. "Absolutely." I walk toward my bedroom with her plastered against my front. "We'll enjoy each other in the meantime."

"I don't want a big wedding. In fact, we should save our money. Med school is expensive."

I set her down next to the bed and pull her pale green dress up and over her head. "That's better." I go for the back hook of her bra. "How's this? We marry in a small civil ceremony before med school starts, so we can afford a honeymoon. Say, two weeks in Hawaii. Jack raved about it."

She gasps. "Did you already plan this too?"

I can't help my smile. "Yup. I didn't want you distracted by all this stuff when you had finals."

"Bren! How did you know I'd love all of that?"

I get her bra off, toss it, and yank her panties down. Then I tackle her to the bed. She squeaks and then laughs.

I kiss her. "Because I know you."

She shakes her head, looking dazed. My awesomeness has that effect on her. "Did you already book the honeymoon?"

"Sure did." I nuzzle into her neck and take her earlobe between my teeth. "Courthouse ceremony in early July followed by Hawaii. We'll be back in plenty of time for the beginning of the semester."

She smacks my shoulder. "Get out! It's perfect!"

I laugh. "I know!"

I get off her just long enough to strip and grab a condom, and rejoin her, lacing our fingers together and pinning her hands to the mattress. Her lips part, her eyes shining with happiness. All because of me.

"You sure were confident," she says.

"I know my woman."

"You do. I'll have to plan something cool for you too."

"You, Chloe, you're the only thing I need."

She frees her hands from mine, grabs my ass, and tugs me closer. I take the hint, sliding deep inside her. Our gazes lock and it hits me this is the first time we're making love as an engaged couple.

"You're looking at me all mushy," she accuses. "Stop it, or you'll make me cry."

"Can't help it." I lean down and nip the side of her neck. "I love you so damn much."

It's different this time, less urgent, but oh-so-satisfying. Our breaths mingle, and we connect on some deep level that's beyond words, beyond our bodies. It's the absolute bliss of true love.

It finally happened for me. She was so worth the wait.

EPILOGUE

Chloe

It's Labor Day weekend, early September, and I've got a few days off med school for the first time in a month. It's a relief to get away. Not that I don't love it, but it's a lot of hard work. I've learned to appreciate my downtime. Brendan and I drove down to New York to meet up with his family at a lake house they rented.

"Text Jack that we're close," Brendan says as he turns onto Lakeshore Drive.

I send a quick text (all of my new Rourke family is in my phone now) before peering out the window, taking in the cute cottages and larger houses up on the hill over-looking a pretty lake with a few people in rowboats and canoes.

"It's so beautiful," I say. "Have you been here before?"

"Yeah. Jack and Riley were engaged here at a lakeside cottage, and they rent one every Labor Day for a family party to commemorate the event. Now that our family's gotten larger, they rented a bigger house." He points ahead. "It's that two-story white house up there."

"Ooh, look at the deck overlooking the lake. That's so nice. I wonder why no one's sitting out there."

"Probably gathered around the food inside. Jack's friend

owns a restaurant in Brooklyn and caters for them every year."

"So fancy."

He laughs and gives my hand a squeeze. "Yeah."

"Have you ever gone fishing?"

"Nope."

"Me either. Maybe we could try it while we're here."

He pulls into the driveway and turns off the car. "Whatever you want. Jack says there's bass and trout mostly."

"No idea what they look like, but I guess I'll find out." I get out and meet him at the trunk of the car, where we packed an overnight bag and a six-pack of beer. I take the beer.

Brendan hauls out the large wheeled suitcase, shuts the trunk, and takes the six-pack from me. He jerks his chin for me to go ahead of him.

"Bren, now I'm empty-handed."

"Bring your biggest smile. Chop-chop. Jack says he left the patio door open on the deck and to come up that way."

I climb the steps of the deck and wait for Brendan by the large wall of glass, peering inside. "It's all decorated with heart balloons, flowers, and white streamers."

"Huh. Sounds like they're celebrating something."

I glance over my shoulder at him suspiciously. He sounds a little too nonchalant.

He grins, his blue eyes dancing with amusement. "Open the door for me, please. My hands are full."

"Is this an ambush?"

He lifts his brows. "As in, the entire family attacks? Sounds about right."

I laugh. I'm being silly. I open the glass patio door and hold it for Brendan. Everyone stops talking to stare at us.

"They're here," someone whispers loudly.

"I thought he was texting Jack when he was five minutes away," someone else whispers.

"Shoot. My phone's charging."

I turn to Brendan, who looks amused and then lifts his brows and nods to his family in a gesture of *let's go*.

"Congratulations!" everyone shouts.

And then the horde descends on us. My father-in-law hands me a bouquet of red roses, my sister-in-law Josie settles a bridal veil on my head, and my mother-in-law gives me a blue garter, which Brendan slides on me while I'm still standing in complete shock. Someone absconded with our suitcase and the beer.

I blink, confused. "Why am I wearing a veil and a garter? We got married two months ago."

Brendan whispers in my ear, "They wanted to celebrate with us here, since we did the small courthouse ceremony. Most of them missed it."

I turn back to my new family in awe that they'd do all this for us. A party for something they missed out on. "We didn't mean to leave anyone out of our wedding. We were trying to save money because of med school and the honeymoon. Oh, now I feel so bad you all missed it."

"Let's recreate it," Brendan says, peeling off his T-shirt.

My jaw gapes at my shirtless husband. "What're you doing?"

He catches another T-shirt that Jack just tossed him, and pulls it on. It's one of those shirts imprinted with a fake tux in front. It's absolutely ridiculous and so fun. I giggle, and then I can't stop laughing.

"I'm matron of honor!" a familiar feminine voice says.

My head whips around. "Sara! Oh my God, I didn't know you'd be here!" My eyes fill, and I rush to hug my sister.

She pulls away and adjusts my veil in her motherly way, smiling. "I wanted to celebrate with you for wedding part two."

"Thank you." I hug her husband, Adrian, who appears at her side. "And thanks for your part in arranging this." I know he's the one behind the scenes arranging everything with the private jet, not to mention getting staff to cover for him and Sara in their absence from the casino.

"You're family, Chloe," Adrian says. "Anything for family."

I wipe my tears, completely flabbergasted by the turn of

events. I jab a finger at Brendan. "You should've warned me. Now I've got the waterworks going on."

He takes my hand. "More fun this way."

"Is that why you told me to wear my white sundress?"

"Yes, and that's also why I bought you the white sundress." He winks. "Plus you look so sexy in it."

I laugh and look around. "Wait, where's Henry?" My nephew is only a month shy of two years old. I can't wait to see how big he got.

Sara smiles. "He's your ring bearer, and Olivia is the flower girl. Ariana is getting them ready behind the island over there." There's an island separating the great room from the kitchen. Olivia is Dylan and Ariana's adorable little girl.

Henry's voice rings out. "Mama!"

"We'd better get started," Sara says. "Places, everyone!"

The space is a large room that's mostly cleared of furniture, just a few chairs against one wall on my far right. I look to my left and there's an arch of pink flowers. I gasp. How did I not notice that before?

Josie pipes up in her loud theater voice. "Do you like it? The arch is from my Valentine's Day wedding. Except we had a lot more pink decorations."

"It's beautiful," I tell her. "Thank you for sharing it."

She rushes over to me, beaming. "No problem. It works well for an indoor wedding with the silk flowers." She kisses my cheek. "I'm so psyched we get to be at your wedding now."

Adrian sets down a red carpet runner, and Garrett helps him roll it out. I've got an aisle to walk down. Unbelievable.

Next thing I know, everyone's in place. This is so nuts. A bride who's already married! Brendan's standing by the arch of flowers, waiting for me with my father-in-law as the officiant. Garrett is the best man. Sara gathers Olivia and Henry at the other end of the carpet runner. Olivia is nineteen months old now. They're growing up so fast!

Processional music starts playing through a speaker set on the island. I join Sara, Olivia, and Henry. I can't stop smiling as I take everyone in. Our family gathers around either side of the red carpet runner. For so long I thought my only family was Sara and now look! So many people who love me and I love back with my whole heart.

Adrian appears at my side. "Would you do me the honor of letting me walk you down the aisle?"

I give him a watery smile and nod. "I'd love that." Adrian has known me my entire life, from my baby days summering on Villroy with my family when we were all kids. He's claimed me as family, and I didn't quite accept that until now. I swallow over the lump in my throat. I have family on two continents. How did I get so lucky?

Henry slams into my leg, hugging me. I peel him off, crouch down, and give him a hug. "I heard you have an important job, big boy! You're going to give Uncle Brendan that pretty pillow and ring." It's a giant red jeweled candy ring. Thankfully, they left the plastic on, or Henry would've tried to eat it. I point him in the right direction. "Go ahead. I'll meet you down there."

He takes two steps and then goes back for his mom. Sara takes his hand and starts down the aisle with him.

Olivia doesn't need any prompting. She's carrying a basket of rose petals and, for a toddler, she's incredibly graceful, sort of dancing down the aisle, stretching her little arm out and flinging a petal, doing a twirl, taking a few steps, and then doing another long stretch and fling.

"Just like her mom," Dylan says proudly. "Little ballerina."

Ariana shrugs. "I didn't teach her that."

Everyone *oohs* and *aahs* over the adorable kids.

The music changes to the wedding march, and suddenly it all feels real. I didn't have a wedding march or a procession for my practical courthouse wedding. Oh, I'm so glad I get the chance now!

Adrian offers me his arm, and I take it.

And then I walk down the aisle to my husband, prepared to marry him all over again.

∾

Brendan

Welp, if she didn't know it already, she does now—my family is nuts. They understood about our courthouse wedding, but they just couldn't help themselves with the reenactment. Since Chloe got on board so easily, I'm going to declare tonight our wedding night part two. She was a wildcat that night.

I grin as she wipes a bit of icing from the corner of my mouth. Everyone's eating wedding cake and drinking champagne. Someone let the toddlers have sugar, and now they're racing circles around the room just for the hell of it.

Chloe spears another forkful of cake. "This was so amazing I think we should do it again. You know, a vow renewal on a cool anniversary, like for our twenty-fifth or something."

"Or how about the tenth anniversary on a beach ceremony in Hawaii, huh?"

Her eyes widen. "I love that. You're awesome at this planning stuff. You're officially in charge of planning cool vacations and all future vow renewals."

I kiss her cheek. It's not that great an honor. She doesn't enjoy planning, all of her focus on her studies. And me, of course. She's only grown more loving and affectionate with each passing day. It's like she had to learn to trust that I was really sticking around like I said I would. I understand. Losing both your parents at a young age can give you serious abandonment issues. It was tough on her.

Dylan guides his huge pregnant wife past us, heading to the patio door. Ariana's due next month with twin girls. They both say three kids is plenty. Dylan is going to be so outnumbered in his house with three daughters and a wife.

"Everything okay?" I ask him.

He smiles. "Everything's good. She just needs a little walk. Getting crowded in there with twins."

"Congratulations again, you two," Ariana says, holding her big belly and letting out a breath. "So happy for you."

Out of the corner of my eye, I spy a blur of long dark hair barreling toward Ariana. I scoop my niece up before she can knock her mom off balance. I turn her upside down. "Where do you think you're going?"

Olivia laughs hysterically as I lift her up so we're eye to eye.

"Careful, Bren," Dylan says. "She just ate cake."

I set her down again, and she grabs onto Dylan's jeans, staring up at me with her big brown eyes and smiling shyly. She's like a mini-Ariana. Dylan plucks his daughter off the ground and tucks her into the crook of his arm. She looks perfectly content, unfazed by the movement. He guides Ariana out. "See ya in a bit," he says over his shoulder.

Chloe turns to me. "Do you ever look at your niece and all your pregnant sisters-in-laws and wish we were having babies sooner rather than later?"

"Nah. All these nieces and nephews will be our practice. Like when you get a puppy to make sure you can keep something alive before the human variety."

She laughs.

I lean down to her ear and whisper, "It does seem like something's in the water around here, doesn't it?" Not only is Ariana pregnant, but Jack's wife, Riley, is seven months along, and we just found out today that Connor's wife, Becca, is three months pregnant. My parents are thrilled. They love being grandparents. Josie and Sean are waiting. She's young and her acting career is taking off. She just landed a sitcom that she stars in. The nice thing is they're filming in New York.

Chloe nudges my shoulder. "It's not the water. It's too much testosterone. All that virility."

"I think it's the women. They can't resist a Rourke."

She smiles up at me. "I'm a Rourke now, so that means you can't resist me."

"And vice versa." I kiss her tenderly. I didn't ask her to, but she took my name. She said she did it so our future kids would share the same name as us. Family is important to her. Still, I can't help but marvel at her willingness to do that. It's such an honor. One day they'll say Dr. Chloe Rourke discovered the cure for cancer. A Rourke will go down in history for something amazing. My woman is going to shake up the world and for the better.

We finish up our cake and head to the kitchen with our dishes. Beast is in there, grabbing a beer from the refrigerator. He straightens, pops the top with a bottle opener, and offers it to me.

"I'm good, thanks," I say. "And thanks for stepping in as my best man again." He was there as a witness/best man at our courthouse ceremony. Chloe's sister, Sara, was the other witness/matron of honor. My parents were there too. I knew they'd never forgive me if they missed it.

He takes a pull on his beer. "You owe me one."

"Sure, sure, when you get married, I'll do the best man gig. Hey, that means I get to plan a bachelor party too."

"Yeah," he says, leaning against the counter. "Just need the bride."

Chloe gives his arm a squeeze. "You're a catch. The right woman will come along."

He grunts. "The *right* one. Now that's the sticking point."

I sock his shoulder. "You're twenty-six. Relax, play the field."

Chloe turns to me. "You were twenty-six when we met."

"Yeah, but we didn't get engaged until I was twenty-seven. And by the time we married, I was twenty-eight."

"By less than a week."

I send her a warning look. Beast is sensitive. She's making him feel bad, being the only single guy here. He's had girl-friends, but nothing that lasted.

Understanding dawns, and she turns to him. "Relation-ships aren't all they're cracked up to be."

"Hey!" I protest. She didn't have to implicate me in that one.

He chuckles and raises his brows at me. "Yeah, okay. Thanks, Chloe."

Chloe sends me a pointed look that says she was just trying to make him feel better.

"You guys have a whole language made of looks," Beast says. "It's freaky."

"Hey, guys!" Josie carols as she walks in and helps herself to a glass of water. "*Living Gold* uses a live studio audience on taping days. You should come. Your parents saw it last week and said they enjoyed it." That's her new sitcom.

"Thanks, but we're heading back tomorrow," I say. "We'll catch it once it airs."

"Do you ever tape late?" Beast asks.

"Sometimes," Josie says. "Call time is anywhere from three to seven."

"Cool. Let me know if you're running on the late side one week and I'll go."

Josie beams. "Awesome! You'll love it. I'll get you on the list with a special reserved seat in the front row. I have to warn you, though, sometimes tapings can take hours."

"No problem. After all, you let me stay at your place rent-free."

"Oh, you!" She turns to us. "He's legit house-sitting for us when we're away and refuses to let me pay him. And he leaves dinner for us the night we get back." She gives Beast's massive shoulder a squeeze. "Such a sweetheart."

She congratulates us again and heads out in search of Sean, her husband. He's over by the floral arch, where they got married almost two years ago now.

Chloe, Beast and I head out to the deck to take in the view. Jack calls for Beast to help with the grill a few minutes later, so then it's just me and my wife, standing by the deck rail, taking in the sparkling lake surrounded by a canopy of leafy green trees.

I slide an arm around her shoulders. "Are you thinking what I'm thinking?"

She looks up at me, a mischievous smile tugging at her lips. "Reenact our wedding night?"

I bend her over my arm for a kiss, and she yelps in surprise. I grin and kiss her before letting her back up. "I knew there was a reason I let you lure me into a committed relationship. You've got a similar dirty mind."

"I lured you? More like you teased and tempted until I

had no choice but to give in because you were so head over heels for me."

I shift her in front of me and wrap my arms around her waist from behind. "Rewriting history, are we?"

She relaxes against me. "Problem is…" She turns around, goes up on tiptoe, and whispers in my ear, "I didn't pack the handcuffs." She's right back to the important thing—wedding night part two.

"How's this?" I manacle both her wrists in one hand and lift them over her head. Then I kiss her roughly.

"That works," she says when I finally let her up for air.

I keep my grip on her, taking in her dilated eyes and flushed cheeks. "I can't wait for tonight."

"Me too," she says in a breathy voice.

"What in the world are you doing to her, Brendan?" my mom asks.

I turn to see my parents standing behind us on the deck. My dad arches a brow in question. Chloe's cheeks are bright pink. I guide her in a slow twirl, keeping her wrists in one hand. "Dancing."

"Interpretive dance," she says with a straight face. It's an inside joke with us. I nearly bust a gut, trying to hold in my laughter.

I take her hand and guide her off the deck, waving to my parents as we go.

We're both dying, trying to hold in the laughter. When we're a safe distance away, she asks, "How red is my face?"

"Better now."

"You think they know?"

"Nah." *Yes.* I'm sure they filled in the blanks. "Jack says any of the rowboats out front are for us. Wanna go out on the lake?"

"Okay."

We make our way to the bank just beyond a copse of trees.

"You row. I'll sit," she says.

"That's not how a rowboat works."

She fondles my biceps. "But you're the one with the spectacular muscles." Then she pins me against a tree, her mouth crashing into mine. Raw lust spikes through me instantly.

She pulls away and smiles, a sweet angelic smile. "Okay?"

"Sure." I can't even remember the question.

A few minutes later, we're in the rowboat, powered by my spectacular muscles while she's sitting pretty up front, facing me and admiring my muscles at work. I wait until we're in the center of the lake before yelling, "Tidal wave!" I rock the boat side to side.

She grabs the sides. "I swear if this boat capsizes, you're going with me."

"Careful, I heard those trout love a light snack."

"Payback!" she yells.

I stop. "Sexy payback? That's the only kind that's worth it."

She crooks her finger at me. I stand and take a careful step toward her. She rocks the boat, and I go flying overboard. *Devil woman!* The water is refreshingly cold. Of course I can't enjoy it alone. I grab the side of the boat and tip her out.

"Ahh!" she screams.

She pops up a moment later and splashes me in the face. Then she swims to the boat. I give her a boost back in—she's a lightweight—but before I can get in, she grabs a paddle and starts rowing away. I spot the other paddle floating away and retrieve it, treading water.

She looks like she's having a blast, suddenly paddling on her own, switching sides on either side of the boat. She's going extremely slow, though, because her muscles can't compare to mine. She doesn't even lift baby dumbbells.

"I can see right through that white dress of yours," I call.

She stops and looks down at herself. "Oh crap. I might as well be naked."

I take that opportunity to swim up, toss the other paddle in, and haul myself into the boat. Then I peel off my soaking wet fake tux shirt and put it on her. Which is not easy, with it being wet, but she helps me as best she can. The black of the tux markings hide the most important bits.

She pushes her wet hair out of her eyes. "I look ridiculous."

"You've never looked more beautiful." And I mean it. There's not a single way I've seen her where I haven't thought she was beautiful.

Her eyes go soft. I drop to my knees in front of her, and she wraps her arms around my neck, pressing her lips to mine.

A long while later, she breaks the kiss. "You see the kind of predicaments you get me into?" she asks, stroking my jaw.

"Here's to many more. Let's get a hot shower together to warm up and take the edge off." I waggle my brows at her.

She smiles, her green eyes gleaming. "We have to be very quiet in there."

I sit back on my seat and commence power rowing. "I can't help it if you're loud."

"You make me loud."

"I simply give, Chloe, I'm a giver. You have to get better control of yourself."

We grin at each other for one sparkling moment, completely in tune, in the middle of a lake on a sunny day with the birds chirping and the gentle lap of the water against our boat. Every moment with Chloe is amazing, but this one is special. My wife for the second time is soaking wet, wearing my groom shirt and smiling at me. My chest aches with all that I feel for this incredible woman.

The moment I get us back to shore, I frame her face in my hands and kiss her. "I love you, wife."

"I love *you*, husband."

And then we walk hand in hand back to the house, looking like two mutts who just took a swim, dripping wet and happy as can be. Mostly because we're about to get very dirty getting clean, but also because of the love. Always the love underneath it all. She's got my heart and I've got hers. Forever.

Don't miss the next book in the series *Rogue Beast*, featuring Garrett in a fake relationship with very real chemistry!

Harper

Everyone thinks I'm tough as nails because I used to play a CEO on TV. I'm not. Unfortunately, it's brought weird stalker men out of the woodwork, which is why I finally broke down and hired a bodyguard. Cut to: a beast of a man with striking aquamarine eyes shows up on the set of my new show. Insta-lust completely takes me by surprise. I'm talking a full head-to-toe rush of heat, fluttering stomach, every nerve ending alive.

This is a problem. I have a boyfriend, and this is supposed to be a professional relationship. I'm lusty as a teenager coming face-to-face with my crush. And then I realize—my crush is into it.

Garrett

I was visiting my sister-in-law on set when Harper Ellis invited me to her trailer. She's a beauty, all right. A little shy and very sweet. We really connected, so I didn't want to spoil the moment by admitting I wasn't her bodyguard.

Her real guard shows up and I figure that's the end of it. Turns out she's got a boyfriend. But then they breakup and the fallout makes people feel sorry for her (the guy cheated on her in a public way). To save face she claims she was seeing me.

I don't care if we're faking a relationship for the good PR, the chemistry is real, and I start thinking we have a future. Until everything blows up in my face. Now I have to prove that we belong together.

Sign up for my newsletter to be emailed when *Rogue Beast* releases at kyliegilmore.com/newsletter

ALSO BY KYLIE GILMORE

**Happy Endings Book Club Series <<the Campbell family and a
romance book club collide!**

Hidden Hollywood (Book 1)

Inviting Trouble (Book 2)

So Revealing (Book 3)

Formal Arrangement (Book 4)

Bad Boy Done Wrong (Book 5)

Mess With Me (Book 6)

Resisting Fate (Book 7)

Chance of Romance (Book 8)

Wicked Flirt (Book 9)

An Inconvenient Plan (Book 10)

A Happy Endings Wedding (Book 11)

The Clover Park Series <<brothers who put family first!

The Opposite of Wild (Book 1)

Daisy Does It All (Book 2)

Bad Taste in Men (Book 3)

Kissing Santa (Book 4)

Restless Harmony (Book 5)

Not My Romeo (Book 6)

Rev Me Up (Book 7)

An Ambitious Engagement (Book 8)

Clutch Player (Book 9)

A Tempting Friendship (Book 10)

Clover Park Bride: Nico and Lily's Wedding

A Valentine's Day Gift (Book 11)

Maggie Meets Her Match (Book 12)

The Clover Park STUDS series <<hawt geeks who unleash into studs!

Almost Over It (Book 1)

Almost Married (Book 2)

Almost Fate (Book 3)

Almost in Love (Book 4)

Almost Romance (Book 5)

Almost Hitched (Book 6)

The Rourkes Series <<swoonworthy princes and kickass princesses!

Royal Catch (Book 1)

Royal Hottie (Book 2)

Royal Darling (Book 3)

Royal Charmer (Book 4)

Royal Player (Book 5)

Royal Shark (Book 6)

Rogue Prince (Book 7)

Rogue Gentleman (Book 8)

Rogue Rascal (Book 9)

Rogue Angel (Book 10)

Rogue Devil (Book 11)

Rogue Beast (Book 12)

ABOUT THE AUTHOR

Kylie Gilmore is the *USA Today* bestselling author of The Rourkes series, the Happy Endings Book Club series, the Clover Park series, and the Clover Park STUDS series. She writes humorous romance that makes you laugh, cry, and reach for a cold glass of water.

Kylie lives in New York with her family, two cats, and a nutso dog. When she's not writing, wrangling kids, or dutifully taking notes at writing conferences, you can find her flexing her muscles all the way to the high cabinet for her secret chocolate stash.

Sign up for Kylie's Newsletter and get a FREE book! kyliegilmore.com/newsletter

For more fun stuff check out Kylie's website https://www.kyliegilmore.com.

Thanks for reading *Rogue Devil*. I hope you enjoyed it. Would you like to know about new releases? You can sign up for my new release email list at kyliegilmore.com/newsletter. I promise not to clog your inbox! Only new release info, sales, and some fun giveaways.

I love to hear from readers! You can find me at:
kyliegilmore.com
Instagram.com/kyliegilmore
Facebook.com/KylieGilmoreToo
Twitter @KylieGilmoreToo

If you liked Brendan and Chloe's story, please leave a review on your favorite retailer's website or Goodreads. Thank you.